# KLITZMAN'S PREDATORS

## By

I0653807

## PAUL BLADES

Other books by Paul Blades:

Klitzman's Isle
Klitzman's Empire
Klitzman's Paradise
Klitzman's Pawn Book One
Klitzman's Pawn Book Two
The Taking of Cheryl Part One
The Taking of Cheryl Part Two: Slaver's Bait
Comfort Girl No. 4
Sacrifice to the Emerald God
The Blue Cantina: Anna's Surrender
The Warlord's Concubine, Books One to Four
Dreams and Desires Book One
Dreams and Desires Book Two
Becoming Ghaniyah

The Maddy Saga:

# PART ONE: PALIBA

## CHAPTER ONE
## A NECESSARY ATTITUDE ADJUSTMENT

You know me. It's Harry, Harry Wiggins. For those who don't, well, suffice it to say that I'm 38, about 6'½", broad shouldered and have a face that used to scare my mother. I'm a fugitive from a life sentence at the Federal Penitentiary in Atlanta, I'm an undercover agent for some secret US governmental organization that I don't even know the name of. I'm a slaver, an enforcer, a saloon keeper, Mrs. Wiggins' not so favorite son and, when all is said and done, really a nice guy at heart. See, that was easy.

In my last missive, I described how my employer, who goes by the name of Klitzman, may he rot some day in the deepest regions of hell, sent me on a mission to the remotest part of eastern Pakistan to bring back a priceless, jade statuette. Klitzman is a 350 pound, evil glutton who runs this bizzaro island resort for the wicked and depraved off the coast of West Africa. He's got his hand in just about every illicit pie you can think of around the globe. My ticket out of prison was a promise to go undercover to take him down.

If I had known the amount of depravity it would require me to witness and take part in, well, I probably would have done the same thing as I did. I mean, where else can you get your cock sucked four or five times every day by the most beautiful, subservient, well practiced female mouths you can think of? Not to mention the great meals, the mostly balmy weather and the company of the world's richest and most depraved men in the world. We even have a nine hole golf course. And except for the depraved men part, you can't get any of those things in prison.

It had been some weeks since I had returned from the Hindu Kush. It had not taken long for me to get back into the swing of things. I had left not knowing if I would ever see my personal slave girl, Carol again. She had been taken away when I committed the faux pas of assaulting an honored guest. Based on my success, she was gifted back to me not too worse for wear. The problem was I had inadvertently obtained ownership of two more, both of whom I had promised to free and who I never intended to be brought back to Klitzman's Isle with me. Annie, a delectable, diminutive, blond American had been kidnapped while on vacation in Nepal and was serving as a whore in a Chinese village deep in the Hindu Kush. Pritha was of Indian extraction and I had purchased her way out of slavery while on our trek to get the dingus. Both were now my personal property.

Pritha had accepted her new fate with equanimity; her conditions of embondment had been quite severe before I liberated her. Being on Klitzman's Isle was actually a step up for her. But little Annie was pissed as hell. Even her training in Rukimo's dungeon didn't knock the rebellion out of her, at least as it pertained to me. I had her serving in the jazz club that I managed on the island. Her principal duties were as a waitress, but not her primary one. Like the other waitresses, who served naked, she was subject to the use of the patrons as the whim struck them. She had had no problem with that, or, at least had resigned herself to it. But when it came to taking orders from me or submitting to my pleasures, she was as ornery as a rattlesnake.

Well, I couldn't let that go on. I had my reputation to maintain amongst Klitzman's staff, for one thing. If they felt I was letting a slave girl get the better of me, my stock would go way down. And I had a bevy of girls to manage, the lounge girls, ones who as a result of their especially beauty and poise were allowed to dress up and pretend they were guests at my club, as well as the other waitresses.

One night, about two weeks after she had emerged from her training, everything came to a head. One of the attractions of the club was a stage where two women were continuously engaged in Sapphic pleasures with one another. It amused the guests and drove their libidos, not that they needed much driving. The girls worked in twenty minute shifts and then went back to waitressing. They would be replaced by two more on a rotating basis.

One of the girls who was due to take the next shift was taken downstairs to the private rooms by a guest. I told Annie to replace her. She had had a shift a little while before. When I gave her the order, her eyes lit up with fire and she told me, "No way! I was just up there an hour ago!"

I was dumbfounded. A couple of the other girls heard her outburst. I had to do something.

It was one of my cardinal rules not to discipline a slave girl when angry. So I held my temper. I took hold of her wrists and clipped her slave bracelets together. I had the bartender give me a slave gag and I ordered her to open her mouth. She must have realized that she had pushed me too far and she started to apologize. Tears were forming in her eyes. It was way too late for tears. I ordered her to open her mouth and I slid the mouth filling gag home, buckling it behind her head. I then dragged her downstairs and fastened her to a hook in my office. She was sobbing by then, knowing that a cruel punishment awaited her.

I left her there until the club closed, about 3 a.m. Normally, all the working girls, those who had not been taken back to his room by a guest, would line up and be chained in a coffle to return to their abodes. The bartender and I gagged and bound their hands behind them. I told the bartender to bring them outside and have them wait for me there.

When I came for Annie, she began to plead and beg from behind her gag for mercy. I ignored her entreaties. Taking a long, thin whip from the wall, I dragged her sobbing form back upstairs and took her outside. Along the way, I grabbed a length of rope.

When we got outside, all the bound and gagged slave girls were waiting. I took the rope and, after attaching it to Annie's bound hands, fastened it to the sign that overhung the door to the lounge. Annie was only about 5'4" and I was able to draw her up until she was on her toes.

I told all the other slave girls to kneel and, when they were all settled, turned my attention to Annie.

She had a delectable body, round hips, beautiful, full breasts. Her blond hair hung down below her shoulders. Her body was glistening with sweat from her fear. She looked at me with eyes agape. They were starry blue and, in her state, piteous to behold. I almost felt guilty about what I had to do. But I knew that it was ultimately in her best interests and in the best interests of all the girls who worked for me. Whatever punishment I was about to inflict would be mild compared to what another supervisor or one of the tall, brawny African security guards would mete out if she or any of the other girls had committed a similar offense in their presence.

I had gotten a reputation as a softie when it came to the slave girls. I rarely beat one for pleasure and I tried to assuage their unfortunate circumstances by acts of kindness when I could. They had to understand, however, that I was a master, after all, like all of the others and was due instant, unquestioning obedience.

Annie began to moan with unhappiness as I swished the instrument of punishment through the air a few times for dramatic effect. It was long and thin and would produce a fiery wound. I turned to the kneeling women. "This is what happens to a slave who is disobedient or who questions an order," I said.

I turned back to my victim. She pulled fruitlessly at her bound hands and was dancing back and forth frantically on the toes of her three inch high, bright red high heels. I heard her moan, "…eeeeeeeeease!" through her gagged lips. And then I let her have it.

The first blow struck her across her plump, rear mounds. It made a sharp slapping noise as it landed. Annie's body went rigid and she emitted an agonized scream. I struck her again cross the back of her thighs. "Aieeeeeeeeeeeeeeeeee!" she screamed. Her gag could not suppress her frantic ejaculations.

The way I had affixed her to the overhead sign there was plenty of room for me to walk around her. She tried to turn her back to me, but the play on her hands only allowed her to turn so far. I laid a blow across her breasts. A bright line of red appeared. "Aiieeeeeeeeeeeeee!" she screamed again.

Tears were flowing like a river down her face. I just kept walking around her and striking her flesh as it became available to me. I delivered a blow across her taut, tender belly, across the front of her thighs, her back and then her breasts again, her rear. She screamed and danced and pulled frantically at her bound wrists.

From time to time I looked back at the other slave girls. The gags they wore had a front piece that covered their faces from their chins to just under their noses, so I could not see their frowns of dismay. But I could see their horror in their eyes. They had never seen me deliver pain like this before. Usually, when I had the need to discipline a girl, I took her down to the basement of the club and whipped her there where she could receive her due in privacy. I very rarely marked them and gave them just enough to make my point. There was rarely a need for a repeat lesson. This was a beating of a wholly different nature.

I stopped after about fifteen or so blows. Annie's body was criss-crossed by bright red lines. She was moaning and crying uncontrollably. I was not done with her though.

I told my bartender, Pete, to go back in the club and bring me back one of the two inch round canes. When Annie heard me give my order, a whole new round of sobs and pleas emerged from her stifled mouth.

"...eeeease, ah-er! ...eeeease, ah-er! ...ooooooo!" she cried out. But no 'please, master' was going to get her out of this.

Pete brought me back the cane and I gave him the whip to hold. While the whip produced a terrible burning sensation when it struck, the cane was a whole different animal. It dug deep down into muscle and flesh when it landed. It caused a kind of body wracking, sickening pain. I rarely used it. But tonight was an exception.

Annie's swaying, beauteous form was highlighted by the spotlight from the sign. A circle of light was cast down around her, like she was a star upon a stage. I heard one of the other slave girls sobbing quietly behind me. Annie moaned, "Oooooooooooohhhhh!" as she looked back at me. "...eeeeeeease," she mumbled plaintively.

I struck. When the cane struck her right thigh, she collapsed. It made a dull, thumping sound when it landed. She uttered a long, low moan of pain. I quickly struck her other thigh. And then her rump. And then her belly. And then the front of her thighs. I reserved the worst blow for last. I reared my hand back and landed one right across her heavy, red laced breasts. She gave out a deep groan and her body collapsed.

I let her hang there for a few minutes. She swayed and

moaned, tears dripping to the sidewalk under her feet. I wanted the other girls to get a good look at her. Although the rule of silence was in force at all times for slave girls, word did get around among them somehow. I knew that the ones present would get word out to the others. I wanted them all to know that Harry was not to be trifled with.

When I untied Annie's dainty hands from the sign, she collapsed to the ground. I gave her a moment and then, prodding her with the cane, ordered her to her knees. She looked up at me, misery on her face. But she did what she was told. I loosened her hands and then fastened them behind her. I removed her gag. She was still sobbing and the sounds of her dismay now became fully audible.

All of the males at the resort wore a standardized robe of various colors. Supervisors like me wore a reddish brown robe, guests, blue. The native security guards wore black ones. I tapped Annie on the side of her face with the cane and opened my robe. My cock was as hard as a steel pole. It was what whipping a slave girl normally did to me. Annie's head was bowed down. Her sobs were subsiding.

"Kneel up and take my cock in your mouth, slave!" I ordered her in the sternest voice I could manage. My voice had normally a grating quality to it and I often communicated more harshness in my commands to the slave girls than I intended. This must have sounded to the poor girl like the word of God.

She snapped her head up and crawled the few feet that separated us. She knelt up and took my prick between her lips. The moist heat of her mouth sent a tremor of pleasure through my body. She began to work it in earnest, massaging my glans with her tongue, driving her lips down its length and back again. She was blubbering with dismay but managed to not let it interfere with her obligation.

I looked at the other slave girls. Their eyes were fixated

on the tableau before them. The significance of the demanded act of subservience was not lost on them. Despite the agony I had inflicted on her, she was still obligated to give me pleasure. My domination of her was complete. I could do with her as I wished. Or any of them.

Annie continued at her task with relish. She daren't disappoint me after the beating I just gave her. When I felt my blood begin to rise, I took hold of the hair on the back of her head and took charge. I pulled and pushed her head rapidly on my cock, piercing her throat on each downward stroke. She let out a series of agonized 'ga's' each time my cock sunk home. I felt my need come upon me. When I felt my cock begin to pulse and dance, I held her head down fast on my loins. She gurgled and moaned while I pumped my spume directly into her belly.

I made sure that I was fully finished before I released her. She drew in a loud gasp of desperately needed air and fell to the ground sobbing. I fastened my robe and turned to the other slaves. "Line up!" I commanded them.

Frantically, all the girls leapt to their feet and assembled into two lines, one for the lounge girls and one for the waitresses. The lounge girls had their own dormitory. The waitresses would go to the common one. When they were all lined up, Pete and I connected their collars with chains so that they formed two coffles. I hung around the neck of the lead girls a tag giving their destination and the amount of time they would have to get there. I made it especially short so that they would have to run, not an easy thing to do on high heels.

Unhappy, frightened eyes looked out at me. "Go!" I yelled loudly. They took off, the lounge girls in one direction, the waitresses in another. I watched them scurry away, their steps carefully timed with each others', their bright red shoes clip clopping on the macadam pathway, almost machine like. They all knew that they would be whipped if they did not make it back to their dormitories within the time allotted.

I looked down at the sobbing, blond haired slave girl. "Up!" I told her.

She rose to her feet unsteadily. Pete dashed into the bar and returned with a leash. I could see from his face that he was impressed with my demonstration.

I hooked the leash to Annie's collar and gave it a tug. I was taking her back to my cottage. Her night was not yet over.

## CHAPTER TWO
## DOWN PALIBA WAY

After her lesson in deportment, Annie's attitude vastly improved. I still detected an itsy bitsy resentment from her on occasion as she stared up at me from her knees, my cock in her mouth. I could live with it. To a large extent, she was entitled.

I was able to spend about six weeks of relative bliss after my return before I was summoned to Klitzman's mansion and provided with new instructions. The big fat guy was, as usual, sitting on his massive couch in his reception room, feasting from a tray of goodies with one hand while the other buried itself in a slave girl's conch.

If it had been up to me, I would have kept things as they were. I had let Pritha be Carol's new companion and the two of them conspired daily on how to delight my senses. I loved to watch them together, the dark brown skin of Pritha's contrasted with Carol's pale covering. From time to time I would sadden as I remembered the unfortunate Mary who had been taken from me and sold to a vicious Cambodian colonel hip deep in the heroin trade. He had once treated her brutally and vowed to come back and buy her. She was only on loan to me. Little did I know that I was merely her caretaker until the Cambodian guy took possession of her. I was sure that she was experiencing hell at his hands. I hadn't forgotten about it and, in fact, had vowed to find some way to free her.

But it was not to be yet. I had to earn my bones again and again with this guy. In his strangely accented voice, Klitzman told me that he wanted me to learn the inside part of the slaving business. He ordered me to fly to this Caribbean island where I would hook up with one of his main guys. From there, I would return to the States and bone up on my new trade.

When I returned to my cottage to break the bad news to the girls, I cursed myself. Despite my ultimate inner revulsion at the whole prospect of female slavery, ok, well, maybe not the whole prospect, I found my self getting deeper and deeper into it as I went along. My government contact, who I knew only as Agent Bederson, had told me to hang on, learn as much as I could. That it would all be valuable some day when it was time to take Klitzman down. He had said that somehow Klitzman had his tendrils deep in our government and we needed to find out who his inside men were so that they could be isolated and punished. Any crimes I committed while on my mission would be forgiven, he said. I hoped to god it was true.

So, I made arrangements for some relatively light duty for my two favorites, Pritha and Carol, while I was gone and turned the running of the club over to Pete. Two days later, I was winging my way back to the Western Hemisphere.

I knew that in many ways, this was another test. Go on the outside, follow orders, don't talk to nobody. I knew also that I'd be so closely watched that Klitzman would be able to give me a fart count when I came back. No chance to contact anyone by phone or face to face. Even dropping a letter in a mail box would be risky.

I decided that I would hold off until I could be absolutely sure that I would not jeopardize my position. After all, what had I really learned? I knew that Klitzman's island was somewhere off the central coast of West Africa. I knew that he operated a landing field somewhere in the jungles of Venezuela. These were already known. But as to the substance of my mission, nothing.

The plane from Klitzman's took me back to the

Venezuelan airfield where there was another plane waiting for me, a light job, big enough to island hop around the Carribean and nothing more. As I got off the plane at the jungle airfield, it was already being refueled and prepared for take off. At the cargo bay, two men were off loading several large cartons marked "Fragile" as well as what I knew to be many pounds of refined, pure heroin. Waiting to board the plane were three business types, probably guests and two meaner looking guys, probably Klitzman's men going back to headquarters for some r&r.

Also standing at the base of the off loading ramp, hands chained behind them, hooded and naked were two dark skinned girls, full figured and round and a third girl, pale and thin, with fine blond pubic hair. They were connected to each other with a chain which ran from the neck of the lead girl to the one behind her and so on. Obviously, they were new recruits to Klitzman's island of hell. The business guys were eyeing them with undisguised lust. But I knew they had been given strict instructions. No touchee, no talkee.

I walked swiftly past the little crowd and followed the direction of one of the ground crew to the waiting single engine job. The pilot waved me in and we took off. I had been on the ground for less than five minutes. Next stop, Paliba.

I sat silently in the plane as we flew into the late morning light. I knew the pilot would be under orders not to gab with me and I certainly had nothing to tell him. What little I could learn would have nothing to do with my mission and could only raise suspicions. The less I talked the better for me. Besides, I was busy thinking to myself about how I was going to complete my mission and what I was going to have to involve myself in on this little trip in order to get back to the island in good graces with the boss.

After about a four hour flight, the pilot banked the plane to the left and began a landing approach. I could see a small field ahead as the pilot spoke to ground control over the radio. We landed without incident and I found myself walking through the small antiquated airport with my suitcase in my hand, looking for my contact. I had been waived through customs after showing my passport and the little courtesy card given to me by Klitzman. The old Klitzman magic was at work.

As I approached the exit from the terminal I heard a feminine voice speak my name. I turned and saw a well, dressed, tall woman, apparently a native, standing about 10 feet behind me and to my left. She had copper colored skin and was dressed in a cheerful flowered skirt, bunched at her waist with a simple, white sleeveless top. She looked to be in her late thirties. Her hair was long and black, falling straight down her back. Very attractive.

"Mr. Wiggins, I'm so glad to meet you." She held out her hand. "I'm to take you to the resort. Please come with me."

"An invitation like that is hard to turn down," I said "Lead the way."

I followed her out to a black limousine which was sitting outside of the airport lounge, watching her walk before me. She had a sway, almost a lilt to her walk, like music. Her skirt came down to just below her knees, giving her a demure air. She opened the door to the rear of the limo and motioned me in. She got in behind me and the limo took off. The windows were tinted. The nameless woman sat next to me and smiled slightly as she returned my gaze. She smelled sweet, like jasmine.

"Drink, Mr. Wiggins?" she asked. I noticed just then a small bar behind the front seat. "A Bombay martini, twist of lemon, is that correct?"

"Absolutely correct," I returned somewhat surprised. I wouldn't have thought that my coming would be so noticed and prepared for. But then again, Klitzman left little to chance. Whoever I was meeting here had probably been shown my dossier, or at least as much as Klitzman thought they needed to know.

The trip lasted about forty minutes. I guessed that there wasn't too much driving that could be done on a small island like this one. Probably smaller than a Manhattan borough with about five per cent of the population, or less. With most of them crowded in the main port, one could have a lot of privacy in a deserted corner like we were apparently heading for. Privacy is everything now, isn't it?

"We are here now, Mr. Wiggins. Please follow me inside the gate." The nameless woman led me out of the car and towards a large gate which was guarded by some pretty mean looking fellows. They looked like they came right off Klitzman's island, which they probably did. The limo driver handed my suitcase to one of the guards as the woman and I passed through the outer gate.

About fifteen feet beyond the gate was a small gatehouse where a very smartly dressed black man, black as coal, stepped out and bowed to me slightly, kind of a salute. "Good evening, Mr. Wiggins, we are pleased to have you here as our guest on Paliba. May I see your passport please?" I gave it to him.

"I will keep this document until you are ready to depart, Mr. Wiggins, I am sure you will understand the need for security. I must also insist on the opportunity to inspect your luggage. It will be returned to you shortly."

"Sure, sure." I said. "Don't worry about it." The woman touched my arm and motioned me to follow her. She led me through a second gate and then up a small walkway to the front door of a large mansion building in the old

Spanish style, red tile roof, two stories and spread out for several hundred feet in both directions. We walked into the front door and into a large hallway. There were several very attractive servant girls standing in the hallway, all wearing flowing, lacy, white cotton skirts down to their ankles and white short sleeve tops of the same material. A thin golden belt, more like a silken cord was drawn about each one of their waists and hung down their sides to about a foot above the floor. Their feet were bare. They were all wearing leather collars sporting a golden colored ring in the front and leather bracelets around their wrists.

The woman who had led me inside spoke quickly to the first girl standing by the stairway, Spanish, I thought, or maybe Portuguese. She spoke to her in a sharp, harsh tone, the voice of command. "This servant will show you to your room," she then said to me. "Please refresh yourself and you will be expected in one hour for dinner."

"Thanks," I said. "And will you be joining us?" I asked.

"Why yes, Mr. Wiggins. I will be there. It is my duty to make your stay with us a comfortable one. By the way, my name is Carla. If you find there is anything you need you should use the phone in your room to reach the central telephone. They will find me and I will do what I can for you."

I nodded and started up the stairs behind the servant girl. She too had that lilting walk that Carla had, her hips swaying gently as she led me up the stairs. I followed her to a doorway about three quarters of the way down the hallway. The door was open and she led me inside. The room was about thirty by twenty with a large canopied bed against one wall. Against the other was a wardrobe and dresser and the door to a bathroom. As I stepped into the room, I closed the door behind us and watched the girl walk over to the wardrobe. She opened it and showed me several summer style suits. The dresser contained underwear, socks and shirts. There were several pair of sandals by the bathroom door. Everything for the worn out traveler I thought. Whoever runs this joint is doing ok for himself.

The servant girl had gone into the bathroom and began to run the tub. It was a large sunken tub, big enough for two people to sit in. The girl turned to me and in one smooth motion stepped out of her skirt and then pulled her blouse up over her head. She had jet black pubic hair which bunched out like a small forest between her legs. Her breasts were not large, but firm and round. Her skin was coffee colored, her eyes as black as her hair which ran down to her shoulders in torrents. Her eyes cast down, she knelt by the side of the tub, her knees apart, hands resting on her thighs, open, palms up. I recognized that, it was the pose of submission. Klitzman had reached out to this small Carribbean isle and instilled his system of discipline and training even here. She had leather bands around her ankles, with a small ring embedded in the side. No mystery as to what that was for.

I let the girl bathe me, soaping me as I stood in the tub, her kneeling outside reaching over to rub my back, my stomach, my legs. She shampooed my hair from behind me while I sat with my back to the edge of the tub on a small ledge. The water was warm, relaxing.

Since the bathroom was carpeted, there was little of the echo of most bathrooms to destroy my reverie as the servant girl rinsed my head of soap and then firmly massaged my shoulders. Gently but firmly she rubbed the muscles in my shoulders and back. She then gracefully stepped into the tub with me and began to rub her hands, then her lips across my chest. I reached my hand up and caressed her head softly as she reached her hands lower, down my sides and into my lap. She grabbed my cock, which rose above the water.

Bending over, she took it into her mouth, moaning slightly. The vibration of her moan tremored throughout my body as she worked her way up and down the shaft. Her tongue flicked over the glans of my cock as she sucked gently but firmly. I was leaning back, enjoying the rest, the pleasure after my long flight. She continued for about five minutes, alternating moaning and licking, expertly bringing me close to the edge of my climax and then back. This girl was a pro. Finally, I could hold back no more and I came, a long, slow, pulsing come, like my dick had been working out for a ten mile run. The warmth of the water spread over me like a wave.

As I finished, the girl gently stroked my balls and licked the come off of the end of my cock. I just lay there as she gracefully rose from the tub and disappeared momentarily. She was back in an instant with a large bath towel and robe. I got out of the tub and allowed her to rub me dry, my legs, my chest, my arms. It was like a standing rub down, the way she rubbed and massaged my body at the same time.

When she was done, she gave me a large white terry cloth robe and then motioned me over to the sink. Laid out there were a razor, shaving brush and mug. She made a motion as if to begin to lather up the brush when I stopped her. I was damned if I was going to let even a beautiful stranger hold a razor to my throat. I did it myself as she watched, kneeling on the floor to my right. When I finished, she preceded me into the bedroom and began to pick up the clothes which were lying on the bed. Apparently while I was in pig heaven, someone had come in and laid out the clothes I was to wear. Having gone this far down the route, I figured I might as well go with the rest of the program.

As I was dressing, or rather, being dressed, there was a knock at my door. I opened it. It was Carla. "We will be having cocktails in about ten minutes, Mr. Wiggins. Please come join us."

"I'll be right there." I replied, "My bath took a little longer than I thought it would. Not that I'm complaining mind you."

"Yes, our servants are well trained. They are very disposed to please our guests. I am gratified that you found this one pleasing."

"Very pleasing." The girl's eyes were downcast as I spoke to Carla. "I hope I get the chance to see more of her."

"Alicia will be pleased to remain here to await your pleasure later tonight. Just chain her ankle to the bedpost. She'll be here when you get back. I'll have her dinner sent up. There is a chain and key in the top drawer of the bureau. The other servants will see to any personal needs she might have while she waits."

"Why thank you, I'll just do that. By the way, does she speak any English?"

"She knows many simple commands in English. We don't find it important that they know more than that. I'll see you downstairs in a couple of minutes."

She stepped over to Alicia, put her hand under Alicia's chin, lifting it up and spoke to her again, swiftly, sternly. Alicia's eyes showed fear as she listened and mumbled a two or three word reply. She lowered her eyes again as Carla walked towards the door. "See you soon," she said to me as she left.

I buttoned my shirt as Alicia brought me a set of gold cuff links from the bureau. She fastened them on for me and then picked up my jacket and held it for me to put on.

No tie in the tropics, I thought. The jacket fit to a tee as everything else had. Good planning.

Alicia, still naked, stood before me awaiting some command. I noticed for the first time a small golden disc dangling between her thighs. She was standing with her hands behind her, wrists on her hips, her breasts thrust out, legs apart. Another Klitzman pose. I watched her in silence for a few moments. She was a vision of subservient beauty. Her downcast eyes were like a cat's, deep and dark, her skin, dark, soft and smooth. I stepped closer to her and reached down between her legs, grabbing the medallion which hung there. I could see that the lips of her labia had been pierced and the medallion hung from a ring which had been inserted through the incision.

I grabbed her arm and pulled her over to the bed where I pushed her backwards onto it. Her eyes widened as her hands fell from her hips to break her fall. I stepped between her open thighs, running my hands along them and up to her hips and back down again to her knees. I then lifted her knees up, pushing her legs up towards her chest. This gave me an unobstructed view of the cleft between her legs and beneath to her ass and the tight ring of flesh that sat below. I could see emblazoned into her hindquarter, an angry red, cursive 'k'.

The girl looked at me with fire in her eyes. This one is not long to her bondage, I thought. She still allows herself to rebel. Grabbing her ankles with one hand, I pushed them towards her head, spreading her thighs further. With the other hand I grasped the medallion and examined the inscriptions. On the one side was inscribed in simple block letters the name Alicia. Above it was a pair of crossed whips, more like riding crops. On the other side a single, cursive k: Klitzman. She belonged to him and probably had never even heard his name. Not that that would have made much difference.

After examining the medallion, I released Alicia's legs and, grabbing her wrist, bade her to stand up again next to the bed. I walked over to the bureau and found a light chain, about 8" long, in the bottom drawer. The chain had small locks on each end with a key in one. I tried the key on both locks and found that it worked both of them. I then returned to Alicia. I took one end of the chain and affixed it to a ring on the bedpost towards the foot of the bed. The other end I locked onto the ring which protruded from the leather band around her left ankle. I put the key in my pocket. I would see her later.

## CHAPTER THREE
## SINS OF THE FATHER

I left my room and walked down the hallway to the central staircase. On the way, I noticed several guards, strategically placed down each hallway. Ready for any emergency. The hallways were wide, covered with a plush red and black carpet. The walls were decorated with various paintings. As I examined each one, I noticed that they all dealt with the female form, nude, partially clothed, engaged in various enticing or otherwise voluptuous poses. Just what you would expect in whorehouse.

When I reached the bottom of the stairs, I saw three servant girls standing by the entrance door, all dressed like Alicia, eyes downcast, hands behind them. There was little or no chance of their leaving by that door, or me for that matter, since it was heavily bolted and locked. Besides, there was Mr. Congeniality outside. The windows were all barred, and since the building was evidently well air-conditioned, the windows were probably kept locked and sealed. "I sure wouldn't want to be here in a fire," I thought.

I was escorted by a slender servant girl with radiant, wavy auburn hair down the corridor to a large door. She motioned for me to enter. I was later to learn that while the servant girls were permitted at times to remain unattended, or even to roam unsupervised throughout the halls or around the grounds, they were expressly forbidden to open or even touch any of the doors. I opened the door and stepped into a brightly lit dining room, a large chandelier in its center, a long table, set with crystal and fine china. There were five men standing around the room, chatting, drinking cocktails. Carla was instructing a servant girl on the far side of the room. She spotted me.

"Oh, Mr. Wiggins, I am glad you are here." She dismissed the servant with a wave of her hand and glided over to meet me. "We are about to take our places for dinner. Please sit here next to the head of the table. I will announce your presence."

I did as I was bade and stepped over to the head of the table and sat down in the seat Carla had indicated. The other men drifted to the other seats. All their eyes dressed left as a door opened on the side of the room. A slender, Hispanic looking man, wearing a flowered, Hawaiian style shirt, white pants and a thin moustache entered the room. His face was contorted into a smile as he looked over at me and approached.

"Ah, Mr. Wiggins, so nice to meet you. I welcome you to our little family." He reached over and took my hand. "Gentlemen, greet Mr. Harry Wiggins, he has joined our company and will be assisting in procurement, isn't that so Mr. Wiggins?" I nodded yes. The other men nodded too. Quite a crowd.

"Mr. Wiggins, I won't bore you with the names of my other guests tonight, you will meet those you need to know more formally later. Tonight, we wine and dine. And talk of course. You have much to learn about our systems and procedures. My name is Diskare, Rene Diskare." He motioned to Carla who was standing by the far wall. She, in turn, motioned to the several servant girls around the room who began to serve dinner. Diskare poured me a glass of white wine from a decanter. The other men dug in. Carla took her place at the opposite end of the table directly across from Diskare.

"So, Mr. Wiggins, are you enjoying your membership in our organization?"

"Well," I replied, "it sure beats my last engagement."

Diskare laughed. "Oh yes, I see what you mean. Many of our associates feel the same way, don't you know. It takes a special type of man to fulfill our organizational needs. Right Pierre?" He spoke to a large, well built fellow to my right.

Pierre looked over, "Yeah, sure, Mr. Diskare. Very special." I had no doubt.

The rest of the dinner was filled with small talk about my trip, my health, my liking for the little servant girl who had played the flute for me in my bath. After about forty minutes, and various delightfully prepared recipes, Diskare motioned again to Carla who in turn motioned the serving girls to clear away the dishes.

Diskare led me and the others into the next room, which turned out to be a billiards room, about 50' long, sofas and easy chairs lining the walls. We entered the room through a pair of sliding doors which a red shirted guard closed behind us after we entered. On the exterior side of the room were several large French windows, running the entire length of the wall from the floor to the ceiling. They led out to what was a spacious garden and a view of the sea below. There was a small bar along the interior wall and, at the other end, in the corner, was a baby grand piano, black, shiny and sleek. In the other corner was a small stage, about 6" above the floor in front of which were kneeling two servant girls.

On the stage, her wrists joined over her head, held upright by a chain which led to the high ceiling, was a graceful looking, wide eyed, unhappy, brown haired girl. She was naked except for a gag which partially concealed her features. Some people had house plants, this guy had girls hanging around the house to admire.

One of the men commenced a game of billiards with

Diskare while two others started a game of straight pool on the other table. The servant girls had gotten up and were handing around a tray of snifters and a brandy decanter. I found an easy chair which gave me a good view of Diskare's game and, out of the other eye, the dish in the corner. One of my fellow diners came up to me.

"My name's Dracovich, but everyone calls me Draco," he said. "You'll be working with me."

"Yeah, well, my name's Wiggins, Harry Wiggins." I shook his hand.

"What's your line Wiggins, I mean, you know, what's your tie in here?"

"What are you taking a poll?" I said. I could see him stiffen.

"Listen fellow, don't do me any favors, okay." He started to walk away. I realized that I had made a blunder. If this was the guy I was going to be working with, I had better not piss him off from the gitgo. I could find my self walking on air at 10,000 feet over the Gulf of Mexico. I decided to mend the fence.

"Listen, I didn't mean anything," I said. "I'm just a little jittery. I mean, when I signed on I didn't really think I'd be going back to the States, you know what I mean. I mean, it's not my favorite vacation spot right now."

"Well, I guess I know what you're saying. It's no picnic, I can tell you that," he replied. "You don't have to tell me anything about your past, I mean I really couldn't give a fuck. It's just that a guy likes to know who he's working with. Live long and prosper, you know what I mean."

I told him that I did. Just then, one of the other men, a small guy with a squeaky voice, the kind that made you wonder whether some people should shut up all of their life, began a high pitched laugh. I looked up and saw him and the two guys who had been playing pool standing around one of the servant girls who was kneeling on all fours on top of a hassock. Her dress was flipped up over onto her back, revealing two fine thighs and a delicious ass. The squeaky guy had jammed a dildo into her ass and was pulling it in and out. Squeaky made some comment and the other two men laughed. He then opened his fly and pulled out his dick. Draco spoke.

"Well it looks like that one's taken. I guess I'll go find a companion for myself and then hit the hay. I'll see you tomorrow. Diskare told me to start breaking you in right away."

I bade Draco goodnight and got up from my chair. I wandered past Squeaky and the two dough boys and walked up to the bar. I refilled my cognac and then stepped over to the stage to take a closer look at the girl who was dangling there. As I walked up, her eyes were on the tableau of Squeaky and the servant girl. As I reached the front of the platform, her eyes shifted to me. I could see confusion and fear in her eyes. Obviously she was not a trained slave. Diskare must be getting ready to break her in. After a moment or two, Diskare appeared at my side. "Very beautiful, no?"

"Very beautiful, yes," I replied.

"There will be a little entertainment concerning this girl later. I would like you to join me."

"I'd be glad to," I agreed.

Diskare motioned to a guard who was standing near the door to the hallway. The guard nodded and stepped over to the platform. "She will be leaving us now, but you'll see her again shortly."

The guard unfastened her hands from the chain and the girl slumped into his arms. She had probably been standing on her tippy toes for a long while. The guard straightened her up and then unlocked her wrists, only to join them again behind her back. Grabbing her hair, he made her bend over until her head was level with his waist and then led her from the room.

"Come with me, Harry and we'll have a little chat." Diskare placed his arm on my elbow and motioned towards the garden. We stepped outside and began to stroll down a flower lined gravel path. I could see the ocean below the 200' cliffs, rising and falling like a vast serpent. The moon shone brightly, strewing its light across the waves like a thousand golden fish wriggling on the surface. A lovely night. A lovely night to be a master.

"Harry, I want you to know that Mr. Klitzman has instructed me to grant you every courtesy. This does not happen often, especially for someone who has not been very long in our organization."

"That's okay," I started to protest.

He waved my protest aside. "I've read your dossier and know all about you. Let me be frank. I am entirely loyal to Klitzman. Everyone who works for him who knows what's best is. But I have my concerns. Are you safe, Harry? What is your game?"

I knew that I was being tested. "Listen Mr. Diskare," I told him, "I was facing the rest of my life in the can, not some country club, super max. Klitzman got me out. This is like a second lease on life for me. I'm not going to fuck that up. As for my appearance here, I'm just as surprised as anyone else. My only guess is that Klitzman wants to recoup some of his investment in me."

"Yes, I suppose you're right, Harry. But let me warn you. The men you will be working with, the men you met tonight. They are also wary by nature. Make no wrong moves. I would like to see you back again."

Now I knew I had done the right thing with Draco. Like any organization, the man on the top could control just so much, especially if he needed the skills and knowledge of the men who worked for him. Draco was liable to give me an irrigated liver if he felt threatened. He would think of what to tell Diskare or Klitzman later.

"And so I will show you some of our facilities. Come inside with me."

We entered a doorway which led to a set of stairs down to the basement of the building. We were met with a steel door on which Diskare knocked softly. A black face appeared briefly at the small glass window in the door and then it opened.

We walked about fifteen feet down a hallway where we were met with another door. This opened much like the first and led us into a long hallway with various steel doors along both sides. We stopped at the first door. Diskare removed a key from his pocket and opened it, waving me in. The room was about 30' by 30', with a large contraption like a kid's monkey bar set in the middle. Along both walls were a series of small cages, about five by five. In three of them there were naked young women, bound and gagged. They looked very unhappy.

"This is one of our training rooms. The structure in the middle is where we usually brand our new acquisitions and affix their discs. You can see that it swivels back and forth so as to put the girl in the required or desired positions. A girl can also be left displayed here so as to teach her openness and obedience."

I looked around. There were various sets of whips, chains and other binding devices hung on the walls around the room. There were no windows and the walls were an antiseptic white. The floor was carpeted. Diskare led me over to one of the caged girls. "This girl arrived just yesterday," he told me. "She is one of the Brazilian girls we like to get. We have agents in the mountains and the jungle where the typical peasant is as poor as the dirt he must farm. Daughters are a liability and are often sold so that the rest of the family can survive. The girls are told they are being sold to husbands in the city. They are thus quite surprised when they are flown out of the country and arrive here. Even so, they are usually passive by nature and easy to train. They also have little or no idea where they are, so escape is not a realistic possibility.

"There are two separate classes of embonded women here. Some, like Alicia, who you met, function as servants around the mansion. Occasionally, I will sell one on to one of our clients as a courtesy. The others are those specifically recruited to either serve the guests of the resort as whores or to be sold on or sent to Klitzman's Island. But I am sure you have seen enough here, let me show you the slaves' rooms."

We left the training room and passed down the hall. Some of the rooms I could see by looking in the small spy holes in each one, contained more facilities for training and disciplining slaves. In one I saw another coffee colored girl splayed back on a small platform, her legs chained to poles on each side, obviously awaiting someone's pleasure. We stopped at a door on the left side of the hallway and Diskare unlocked the door and stepped in. It was a long, narrow room with a row of beds along one wall. Above each bed was a ring and a chain which led from the ring down onto the bed into a little pile. A matronly looking woman was sitting on a chair at the end of the room, knitting of all things.

"The servants are under the direct control of Carla, the mistress of the house. They are rarely admitted to the main areas, but both administer to the needs of the slaves and maintain their discipline and order. They ensure that the girls clean and dress themselves properly and are presented for duty when they are needed." He nodded to the woman who just smiled and continued sitting. Only then did I notice that there was a small, naked, light skinned girl at her feet. She was hooded and had her wrists bound to her ankles. A chain ran from her neck to the matron's lap. Slave discipline.

We left the dormitory and Diskare led me down the hall to another steel door. He knocked lightly and it sprung open. "Now for our entertainment," he said.

The room we now entered was a relatively small one. In it were three guards, lounging around several easy chairs which were lined against the interior wall. In the middle of the room was a black leather divan. On it sat the girl from the billiards room. She was dressed now and someone had freshened her makeup. She was sitting there demurely, her knees together, her hands in her lap. She was wearing a light blue blouse with swaths of yellow strewn across it. Her skirt was of matching design and was short, but loose. She was also wearing high heels that matched.

She looked up as we came in and I could see by her red eyes that she had been crying.

"This is the daughter of a high official of the government of a local country where we have extensive interests. He has broken his word to us regarding a very special project. Tonight we will exact our revenge and ensure that it will never happen again.

"We will conduct our little performance tonight in English, which the girl understands fluently. So you will be able to follow along. It will be most amusing for you." Diskare spoke briefly to one of the guards while I regarded the girl sitting before me. I didn't know exactly what Diskare had planned, but I knew it wasn't good. I doubted that this girl had any inkling of what lay in store for her.

After a moment, two more guards entered the room,

both carrying portable video cameras. Like the other guards, they were dressed in red t-shirts and white canvas pants. Diskare motioned to the three original guards who stirred themselves from their chairs. One of them turned down the lights on the sides of the room leaving a small spot glaring into the center, about three feet from where the girl was sitting. The show was about to begin. Diskare stepped about two feet away from the spot on the floor and spoke to the girl.

"Get to your feet," he spat out harshly. She looked up at him, startled, and slowly rose from the couch. Her arms were wrapped around her chest as if to comfort herself.

"Stand in the light," Diskare ordered.

The girl looked at him again as if he were speaking Greek. "Now!" Diskare barked. The girl jumped at the booming sound of Diskare's voice. She placed herself in the center of the light. I saw the cameramen step forward on either side of Diskare and begin to shoot.

"Hands at your sides, stand straight," Diskare barked. The girl stiffened. The three original guards had donned masks which covered the top part of their faces down to their mouths which was left free. There were holes for their nostrils and eyes. The masks, which were black like their uniforms, made them appear ominous, sinister. For a moment the room was silent. The girl took in her surroundings, wide eyed, confused. There was still enough light in the rest of the room for her to see what was going on. I'm sure it was not of a nature to comfort her.

I hadn't gotten a good look at the girl's face before since it was covered by the gag. Her features were as refined as her body had been graceful when I saw it upstairs. She was young, not over twenty two, I guessed. Her lips were full, painted red, and they trembled as she stood there in the silence awaiting the next command. She had been, no doubt, already counseled not to speak unless spoken to. This did not prevent a small whimper escaping her lips.

The silence continued for about two more minutes as all in the room regarded her. The cameramen continued to shoot, getting a good leader for their little film. Then Diskare spoke again.

"You are Marissa Villejo?"

"Y,yes." she stuttered back.

"You are the daughter of Carlos Villejo?"

Her reply was quieter, almost a whisper, "Yes."

"What is your age?"

"Twenty two."

"You have sisters?"

"Y,yes." her voice raised slightly, querulous.

"What are their names and ages?"

The girl looked around. It was obvious that refusing to answer was not an alternative. Besides, she had been plucked from her daily life, transported to an unknown place apparently a thousand or more miles from her home, kept prisoner and paraded naked before unknown men. She had to know that these were questions to which the answers were already known.

"Veronica, twenty, and Luisa, eighteen."

"Today it is you who have been brought here to atone for the offense of your father. He has betrayed those with whom he had bargained. He has lost his honor and now must suffer a punishment. You are to be the vehicle of that punishment."

The girl followed Diskare's words wide eyed, unbelieving. "You have been brought here so that you, with your life, can both serve as compensation to those who have been damaged and serve as a warning to your father that he must not betray those who have bargained with him again."

She began to sway slightly with fear. A tear rolled out

of the edge of her eye and down the side of her face.

Diskare continued. "We are making this record of our proceedings tonight so that it may be shown to your father that because of his dishonor, you are now lost to him. Should he choose to betray us again, it is your sisters, Veronica and Luisa who will stand here where you do today."

The girl began to cry softly.

"Tonight, from this moment, you are to be transformed. You are to be reduced to a vessel, a chattel. From today forwards, you no longer the master of your life, your body. Those things are to be taken from you and to become the possessions of your masters.

"Your mind and your will are to be dedicated totally to the task of serving and obeying those who command you, those who will own you."

The girl's crying became louder. She closed her eyes as if to ward off the words she was hearing. She was shaking violently as the tears poured down her face. Diskare paused for a moment to allow his words to sink in, both to the girl and to the distraught father who was to see this video.

As the girl stood there sobbing, one of the cameramen crept up on the right to get a close up of the girl's face from the side. The other was shooting over Diskare's shoulder.

Suddenly Diskare bellowed "Silence!" The girl's eyes sprung open. She looked at Diskare, terrified. She would as much disobey his commands as put her hand in a meat grinder. She probably didn't know much about what was going on, but what she did know was that she was absolutely at the mercy of this madman who was addressing her, and that whatever he decided would be her fate would happen. She stifled her sobs.

"You will now disrobe," Diskare told her.

She had been naked before in view of these strange

men. But now there were the cameras and her father. For a moment she considered her options: none. Diskare stared into her eyes. Tears streaming down her face, she slowly raised her hands to her blouse and began to unbutton it. When she finished, she drew it down her arms and let it fall to the floor. Her breasts full and round, sprung free. Her nipples were dark and large, like blood red pesos. They were large for her frame, but were graceful and well shaped.

She then fumbled with a zipper on the side of her skirt and then let that fall to her feet. Obviously she had been permitted to don only her skirt and blouse, as she was naked beneath her skirt as well. Her belly was flat and firm, her thighs well toned, tanned. There was the faint hint of white on her breasts and on her lower belly. She had apparently been too demure to expose those areas to the sun. She would have her chance now.

"Kneel!" Diskare commanded. She knelt as the three masked guards now came forward. One was carrying a small carved wooden box in both hands as another approached and drew the girl's hair from around her neck. Then third guard then pulled a leather collar from the box and affixed it around the girl's throat. It clicked shut, a sound as final as death.

"With this collar, you are enslaved," Diskare told her. "You have no name. You have no property. You are not a person, but a thing, to be disposed of as the desire of those who own you shall be."

Diskare motioned to the guards who pulled the girl to her feet. Quickly they attached leather bands to her ankles and wrists. She looked on disbelievingly. Diskare spoke again.

"Now you will learn the terms of your bondage. From this time on your sole purpose is to serve and obey. You will serve through the use of those parts of your body as your masters desire to possess. Your sex, your mouth and your portal behind will be opened and will remain open at all times and to all persons who desire you. As a symbol of the fact that your body is not your own, you are forbidden to touch it except at the command of a master. You will not close your mouth or your knees. These must remain open, ready to serve and to please. Your voice and your thoughts are not your own. Therefore, you will remain silent at all times except when spoken to. And then you will speak honestly and without hesitation, revealing all that is demanded. You will not look at your masters in the face. Who commands you or uses you is no concern of yours. Do you understand?"

This last question set the girl off. She stared wide eyed at Diskare and screamed. "Oh no, please don't do this to me! I have done nothing! Please! Please!" She fell to her knees and lunged out to grab Diskare's legs. Two of the guards caught her by the arms and pulled her to her feet. I could see the sweat glistening on her chest and under her arms, the sweat of fear. She hung limply in the arms of the two guards.

"First you will learn to obey."

The girl was dragged to the other end of the room where a hook and chain was hanging from the ceiling. In an instant the girl's wrists were joined together and connected to the chain. The third guard pulled it taught until she was suspended in the air, the tips of her pale blue shoes barely touching the ground. The cameramen took it all in. Diskare, who was careful to remain out of the shots, stepped up to the girl as her ankles were attached to two pillars which sat on either side of the chain. She was spread-eagled in the air, her body swaying gently back and forth. The lights were adjusted to concentrate on her as the cameramen jockeyed for position. One of the guards approached her holding a whip of several strands, each with a knotted end. The girl stared at it in disbelief.

"Through the pain you will now feel, you will learn that obedience must become your polestar, your imperative. You will also learn that your body is a vessel, a vessel possessed not by you, but by your masters who may dispose of it as they see fit."

He motioned to the guard holding the whip.

When the first blow landed across the girl's back, her eyes popped open and her body jolted. At the second blow she began to cry out. At the third and fourth she began to scream, begging, pleading for mercy. Ten blows were landed, ranging from her back to her ass and the backs of her thighs and calves. The guard took his time, gauging her recovery from the blow before, ensuring that each one was felt separately from the previous. When he finished behind her he paused for a minute to let her catch her breath. She continued to cry and moan, swaying back and forth in her chains. When she had begun to recover herself, the guard came to her front, and as she saw that that part of her was not to be spared, her cries began anew.

"Oh no, please, for all that is sacred, please don't do this to me, please! Oh Papa, Papa, oh, please help me!"

There was no help for the girl. The blows rained on her front as they had on her back, each one raising a spray of red tracks across her skin. Her breasts were first, then her stomach and the inside of her thighs. Only her face and her sex were spared. After ten blows were landed, the guard stopped.

The cameras kept shooting as the guards and Diskare withdrew to take a breather. The girl was slumped in her chains and whimpering. Diskare poured us all a drink at a small bar in the front of the room. While we were sipping our drinks and taking in the spectacle of the flayed girl suspended in air before us, one of the guards started a fire in a small brazier. I knew what that was for.

The girl's whimpering got louder and Diskare spoke to the guard next to me, "Let's put a sock in that."

"Yes, Mr. Diskare," he replied as he went to the cabinet against the wall and pulled out a gag. He approached the girl from behind and, grabbing her hair behind her head, quickly rammed home the gag before the girl knew what happened. He buckled it behind her head and then ran his hands down her front, grabbing her breasts and squeezing them, rubbing the nipples with his thumbs. The guards with the cameras had set up tripods so they could keep their film rolling as they joined us for a drink. All this excitement really built up a thirst. Actually, I think it was more a desire to delay and extend the proceedings than anything else. My cock was hard as a steel rod as I sipped the cognac Diskare had given me. I know I needed a rest.

After about fifteen minutes, Diskare got up and told the guards to get ready for the next phase in this new slave's initiation. The cameramen took up the cameras and the three guards converged about the hanging girl. One of them loosened her ankles as another slowly lowered the chain that held her wrists to the ceiling. She slumped as the chain was lowered until she was on her knees, her hands still suspended over her head. Diskare was holding the whip in his hands as he spoke to the girl.

"Slave," he said quietly.

Her eyes came to attention. She looked Diskare in the face, and then, apparently remembering his previous instructions, looked away, down at the floor, at his feet. "Knees apart, back straight," came the command.

She complied readily. Diskare motioned to one of the guards who proceeded to remove the gag. "Have you learned to obey?" Diskare addressed the girl.

"Yes, yes, please, yes, please don't hit me again, please..."

"Silence! You are only to answer the questions I give to you. No more, do you understand?"

"Yes!" the girl whispered back desperately.

"And you will answer by saying yes, Master or no, Master, do you understand?

"Y,y,yes, Master."

"Now have you learned to obey?"

"Yes, Master."

"Good, now you will learn to serve. Get to your feet."

The girl quickly stood, pulling herself up by the chain.

"Feet apart, wider," Diskare told her. The girl obeyed. A guard grabbed her wrists and loosened them from the chain. Her wrists were then undone.

"Put your hands behind your head," she was told.

The girl looked at Diskare's face momentarily and then flitted her gaze back to his feet. She placed her hands behind her head, raising her elbows parallel to the floor. I couldn't help wondering to myself if the organization would have followed this particular means of revenge against her father if she had not been so beautiful. I doubted it. But then, she might be dead. I wasn't sure which of those alternatives she would pick now.

The large guard stepped up to the girl and ran his hands along her breasts. I stepped to the side for a better view. I could see the girl tense. She knew was what up. She had seen the servant upstairs being plowed by the guy with the grating voice. If she were smart she would just let it happen. It was going to happen anyway.

The guard had fastened his mouth to her left breast. His right hand slid down her side to her thighs and slipped between them. The girl's eyes were crammed shut. The guard moved his mouth to her right breast and began to stroke her sex. I could see that he was burrowing his finger deeper and deeper into her. She made a little squealing noise and squirmed slightly.

"Keep your mouth open" Diskare snapped. Her mouth dropped open. "And open your eyes." She did so, her eyes glistening, darting around the room, seeking to find a place to rest where she would not have to see her own debasement reflected in hard, cruel eyes. The guard looked over at Diskare and smiled. He was now easily moving his fingers in and out of her pussy. He straightened up and grabbed the girl's face with his free hand. His mouth covered hers. I could see his tongue darting in and out. The cameras were still going and the one guard zoomed in on the girl's face. The guard then moved behind the girl, wrapping his arm around her front massaging her breasts. The other he ran between her legs from behind, and from the little jump she made, I could tell that he had launched an assault on the other portal. The girl's face wrenched as the guard pressed his way into her ass.

Diskare spoke, "You must tell me truthfully, are you a virgin?"

"N,no," she whispered.

"That's, 'No, Master.'"

The girl cringed at her mistake. "N,no, Master," she said dismally.

"How many men have you had?

"Two, Master."

"Did you take them or others into your mouth?"

She looked at Diskare dolefully, tears in her eyes and then at the camera. "Y,Yes, Master," she finally said. It must have been difficult for the girl to talk with a hand up her ass. But I guess it would have been hard under any circumstances. Diskare signaled for the large guard to step back.

"You will now get on your knees, back straight, no, not on your haunches, straight up." The girl obeyed and knelt on the floor, her hands still behind her neck. Diskare undid his belt and approached the girl. "You will now take my cock into your mouth and suck it as you have done to your lovers."

The girl looked around the room, stopped at the cameras which were now focusing in on her lips and Diskare's cock. She started sobbing softly as she knew that this scene would be preserved, shown to her father and others. She hesitated momentarily, looked at the whip still lying in Diskare's hand and then opened her mouth and took in his cock.

She worked her head back and forth slowly as she stifled her sobs. The cameraman on the left shot up closely to where cock and lips were joined. I could see Diskare grinning as he took satisfaction from the warmth of her mouth, the feel of her tongue. He let her go on for about two minutes and then placing his hand on her forehead, slowly withdrew.

He nodded to the three guards who then pulled the girl to her feet and brought her over to the divan. She was thrown down on it and her wrists affixed to the ring above her head. The first guard mounted her face to face, slipping his cock into her now juicy quim. She murmured briefly as he took her mouth. He worked at her slowly, steadily as the rest of us watched. The next guard turned her over and drew her to her knees. He penetrated her from the rear and grabbed her breasts which hung down from her chest like two ripe melons. Her face was contorted as the guard plowed away, rocking her back and forth. She was sobbing heavily.

When he finished, the last guard took his turn taking first her cunt and then spilling himself into her mouth. The girl whined and her body squirmed as the man, his knees on either side of her face, plunged his cock remorselessly back and forth between her lips.

Diskare, who had donned a mask, now approached the girl and spoke. "I will now enter the last portal of your virginity. From today, this part of you will become as available as the other two to serve your masters' pleasures."

The girl was lying on her back. Diskare pulled her knees up towards her head, exposing the double cleft below. He slipped into her pussy momentarily and then, holding her ankles together with his one hand and holding his cock with the other, rammed it home into the hole below. The girl cried out in pain, biting her lips, trying to squirm free. Diskare pushed against her with his weight and held her pinned to the divan. He grinned beneath his mask and then slowly worked his hips up and down. The girl's squirming stopped, her cries reduced to moans. After a few moments, Diskare gasped, and expended himself.

He rose from the girl and motioned to me. I was handed a mask by a grinning guard and I stepped forward. The girl was limp, her legs falling on either side of the divan. I rose onto the divan and glided my cock into her pussy. She was hot and tight. My cock was aching with need to explode. The girl's eyes opened, looking at my face briefly and then away. I took her mouth and sucked at her tongue. I hoped the little black guy didn't have anything, but my passions were so strong, I didn't care. I wrapped my legs around the girl's clasping her thighs tightly around my cock. My passions had been on a boil during the entire proceedings and it didn't take much to get me over the top. I groaned, my hips pounding relentlessly into hers as my cock throbbed and jerked in her steamy tunnel. In a minute, I was done.

As I finished, I realized that I had now become a part

of Klitzman's or Diskare's or someone else's revenge against this poor girl's father. I had let myself wreck havoc on her, debase her, without a moment's hesitation. Sure, on Klitzman's island I had done as much. But there, somehow, I had felt protected, protected by my need to get close to Klitzman, the need to recover the information vital to my mission. Here, I had become caught up in an act totally unnecessary to my cover. Or had I?

While the two cameramen took their turns at ravishing the young girl on the divan, I poured myself another cognac and sat in one of the easy chairs by the door. I thought that, on the other hand, if I had not taken part, if I had refused or made up some excuse, Diskare would have certainly been suspicious. He was already suspicious, as he had already told me. Nothing I had done would appreciably increase or affect this poor girl's misery or that of her father and family at her disappearance.

On the other hand, as I wound my way through Klitzman's organization, as I came closer to uncovering his organization's hold over our government, its perversion of our way of life, the closer I came to freeing this girl and all the captive girls like her. Certainly, when the day came that I was able to smash Klitzman, I would be able to lead the authorities to all of his little private hells like this one and burst them open, letting the misery and suffering that was in them escape. I resolved that I would do whatever I could, whatever was necessary, even seeming to be as cruel and as callous as the worst of Klitzman's men in order to complete my mission and destroy Klitzman and his empire.

In the meantime, the cameramen had finished their fun with Marissa. They were relaxing themselves at the bar while two of the guards amused themselves abusing the girl by running the strands of the whip up and down her body. She whined and sobbed, her body flinching each time the strands of leather touched her. The third guard was on the side of the room, stoking the brazier and checking the heat of the iron sitting over it, the branding iron which would soon lick this girl's skin, marking her forever as one of Klitzman's properties. It would mark this night forever in her mind, as if being violated by several men wasn't a mark enough to endure. The kiss of the branding iron would put a seal on the night's events just as much as a kiss between a bride and groom sealed their vows. But these vows, the vows to obey and to serve, short of a miracle, one that I hoped I could provide, would never be broken.

The guard at the brazier spoke softly to Diskare. I understood this to mean that the branding iron was now ready.

I had seen this before, of course, but tonight, because of my doubts, my fears of being lost in this hellish world of Klitzman, my guilt about my actions, I pledged, that this kiss of red hot iron to flesh would also seal my vow to do whatever was necessary to bring Klitzman down.

The cameramen went back to their cameras as Diskare motioned to the other two guards to get ready. Marissa was no longer crying or whimpering, but was lying listlessly on the divan, her eyes staring into space. She had been made numb by her sufferings here tonight. But that numbness was about to come to an end. Diskare lingered a moment and took in the girl's reverie. The guards lined up again in a small circle around the girl. The cameras started to role. Diskare spoke to the girl.

"You have learned what it is to obey and now what it means to serve. There is one final lesson for you tonight. One which will burn into your mind the finality of your enslavement, its permanence, its totality."

The girl was startled to hear Diskare's voice again. Each time he had spoken a new and increasingly terrible blow had been struck against her psyche. She began to whimper anew, too afraid to cry out, to beg. Her fear was like a siren ringing throughout the room.

One of the guards unchained her wrists from the end of the divan above her head and unbound her wrists from each other. For a moment she was unfettered. She seemed lost, confused, and then, at the same time as two of the guards grabbed her wrists, turned her to her belly and began to lash them to the legs of the divan, she saw it. The third guard was carrying the brazier which held the branding iron over to the divan. One of the cameramen followed his approach while the other got the reaction shot. Her face cringed in anguish; her whole body shuddered as she came to understand the meaning of Diskare's words. What was to be burned into her mind was first to be burned into her flesh.

Ruthlessly, the two guards pulled the girl's arms down to two small rings on the bottom of the legs of the divan. Her arms were thus pulled taut, her chest tight against the divan. Frantically, she pushed her legs against the floor, spread on the two sides of the divan, trying to push herself off to win, even momentarily, her freedom.

"Please don't burn me, please!" the girl shouted, her voice carrying the tones of her hysteria. "I'll do anything! Please! I'll be good! I'll do whatever you say! Please! Please!"

Her supplications were ignored. And her efforts to avoid her fate were futile as the two guards who had held her arms quickly grabbed her ankles and bound them to the other two legs of the divan. From under the divan they drew out several straps which they used tie her torso flat onto it. In a moment the girl called Marissa would exist only in a memory, a memory which would divide the time before from her life to come by this moment, this instant.

Diskare moved to the front of the divan and grabbed the girl's face, straightening it, forcing her to look into his own, masked visage. He spoke. "By this mark you will be known for what you are."

At the same instant, the third guard lowered the iron, white hot on its ends, onto the space just below her right hip, about two inches down and a little over. The girl's flesh hissed as the heat of the iron burned out its moisture. A small cloud of smoke rose up as her body jolted. A piercing scream, haunting, reaching out from the depths of this girl's soul, a throaty scream, tailing off at the end, flooded the room. Mercifully, the girl fainted.

One of the cameramen had been able to shoot her face and the kiss of the iron at the same time due to the slight upwards incline of the divan at its head. He waited a moment, allowing the camera to take in the contrast of her now peaceful, sleeping face, to the screaming, anguished face which had preceded it. The other cameraman had taken in the whole of the meeting of the iron with her flesh, and when the iron was removed after the recommended three seconds, took in the vicious, angry scar it left behind. The cursive k, leaving no doubt whose act this was.

The guards and Diskare rose, not breaking the silence which now lay across the room. The girl had soiled herself and the room reeked with a mixed smell of her waste and burned flesh. More drinks were poured as the girl slowly regained consciousness, moaning, straining lightly at her bonds. The thin guard approached her and anointed the scar with the red colored salve which would tint it. Gradually, the men in the room began to talk and exchange light banter about their recent victim.

Diskare picked up a phone located on a table near the door and spoke briefly and quietly into it. A few minutes later there was a knock on the door. One of the guards pulled the door open and admitted two servant girls followed by Carla. Diskare tossed his head towards the girl on the divan and Carla spoke sharply to the two servant girls. They proceeded to the divan where they began to clean up the mess we had made there. Marissa's arms and legs were freed from the legs of the divan by the guards and one of the girls wiped her clean, carefully avoiding the burned tissue above her ass. Carla pulled from the cabinet on the wall a large bandage which she then affixed to the wound on Marissa's backside.

Diskare watched silently. Marissa, supported by the two masked guards at her sides, hung limp, exhausted, crushed by what had happened. As the servant girls finished their tasks, one of the guards took Marissa's wrists and joined them together before her and then, by a small chain, fastened them to the ring in the front of her collar. She was brought before Diskare and pushed to her knees. Diskare regarded her. No cameras this time. He grabbed her face. "Learn to serve, learn to obey," he said. He released her and nodded to Carla.

Carla was holding a leather mask, more like a hood which she pulled over Marissa's head. A gag affixed to the interior of the hood was forced into her mouth and the bottom was pulled tight around her neck. Carla adjusted the front of the hood, assuring that the holes for the girl's nose were in the right place, and then pulled tight the straps in the back of the head. From a pocket in her dress she pulled out a chain which she affixed to the clasped wrists and pulled Marissa to her feet. Pausing only to nod slightly at Diskare, she yanked the chain tight and then led Marissa from the room. Marissa stumbled slightly as she was forced forward and then plodded out the door, undoubtedly to spend the night in one of the cages I had seen earlier.

"Well, that's a night enough for me," Diskare said as he downed his drink. "I shall retire. Harry, you are welcome to use the game room facilities upstairs, but I warn you, we have an early day tomorrow, much work."

"I'm with you Mr. Diskare," I said. "Besides, I've got a little package waiting for me up in my room. I think I'll let her relieve me of some of the heat you've built up here tonight."

Diskare laughed and slapped me on the shoulder. "Very good my friend, very good. Let us go."

We left the basement and returned to the ground floor and then climbed the stairs to the second. "Your room is to the left, Harry;" Diskare told me. "My chambers are to the right. Have a good night."

I thanked him and walked back towards my room. My footsteps echoed down the empty hallway.

# CHAPTER FOUR
## A GIRL MEETS HER DESTINY

On my second day on the island, Diskare invited me to accompany him on a trip to the main city of Paliba, called by the same name. "We're having lunch with a client," was all he said. As a result, we sailed down the winding road towards the city in his limousine. The countryside was lush but obviously poor. We passed one or two villages of cardboard and corrugated iron huts, the denizens hanging about, seeming fixtures gathering dust. Undoubtedly these villages served as a fertile recruiting ground for staff at Diskare's resort. Few of the men of these villages would have any hope of improvement in their lives and would show unswerving loyalty to a man who could do for them what was otherwise impossible. Besides, the fringe benefits of working for Diskare were obvious.

We hit the city after about thirty five minutes of high speed driving and parked in the courtyard of a Spanish style building settled in a rather quaint section of the city. The courtyard was completely surrounded by the building and three walls. A uniformed doorman let us in through a wrought iron gate. Diskare led me inside to a restaurant where a maitre'd escorted us to a table near the back of the room.

The restaurant was sparsely filled, almost empty. At the table was a late fortyish, heavyset man and what appeared to be his daughter. The girl was tall and slender in a graceful, wispy sort of way. She was wearing a white cotton blouse splashed with large, pastel yellow flowers and a long, tan skirt which ended about mid-calf. Demure, and classically beautiful, good fortune dripped off of her in the form of a pair of exquisite pearl earrings which hung like teardrops from her ears and the sparkling string of pearls which looped down from her shoulders and around her neck. Her blouse had a rounded neckline which left exposed the very tops of her breasts, hinting at the fullness beneath. Her long, straight, light brown hair was held back by a yellow ribbon, bowed at the top of her head. She was wearing dark sunglasses, not entirely inappropriate for the brightly sunlit room.

"Ah, Simon, I am glad to see you," Diskare said to the seated man. "And your stepdaughter, yes, so glad to meet you." Diskare held his hand out to the girl. Looking slightly offended, the girl extended her hand limply, touched Diskare's and then dropped it to the table. She looked away.

"My friend, Harry," he said by way of introduction. I shook the man's hand and then the cold fish's.

The man spoke. "Yes, this is my stepdaughter Audrey, Audrey Abrams. I am glad to be able to finally present her to you." Oh, oh, something was up.

"Yes, I'm very glad to meet her; you've told me so much about her," Diskare replied. "I'm so happy you were both able to stop and have lunch with me here. You just totally surprised me when you called." He had the ability to diminish his appearance at will. What I knew to be a cruel, barracuda like sociopath could come on like a hairdressing, weak-kneed pantywaist. All he needed were painted fingernails and a lisp and you'd swear you saw him lilting down Seventh Avenue. He was really pouring it on now. We sat down and Diskare quickly ordered food for us all. "I know all the specialties," he said. And to the girl, Audrey, "Please, remove your glasses. Simon has described your eyes as being quite exquisite and I'm dying to see them."

"Yes my dear, let him see your eyes," Simon implored.

Audrey removed her glasses with a scornful wave of her hand. "I don't see why you can't just leave me be, Simon. I am sure your friends are very nice, but I really want to just have lunch and then get off this dumpy island."

Well, I had just learned two things about this girl. One, if she thought that Diskare and I were "nice", she was a piss poor judge of character. Secondly, I felt that her stay on Paliba was going to be a little longer than she imagined. Oh, and third: her eyes were beautiful.

"Oh, I am sorry if I have troubled you, Miss Abrams," Diskare spoke. "It's just that I am intrigued by Simon's description of you. I feel as if I know you."

"And what has he told you? I'm afraid I don't approve of my stepfather trying to pimp me to his friends," Audrey snapped back.

"Don't mind Audrey," Simon said. "She's upset about our little detour here. We are on our way to the Caymans to celebrate her 21st birthday in two days. At that time she is to come into her mother's estate. I'm afraid all I'll be left with is a small allowance. You see I'm really the one with the right to be upset."

"Simon, I really don't appreciate you're involving your friends in my personal affairs," Audrey interjected. "If you can't discuss something else, I'll go wait at the dock."

"Oh all right, Audrey," Simon said. He looked at Diskare ominously.

Our food was brought to the table by a young servant girl. She was dressed in the manner of the servant girls at the resort and wore the telltale leather anklet around legs, noticeable only to those who knew their meaning. So this little Spanish rendezvous was actually part of the club. That explained the iron gate, the doorman and Diskare's presence here. I knew that Audrey was in for quite a surprise.

The restaurant filled up with several groups of very classy looking people, the kind who drank in money every morning and exuded wealth and privilege the rest of the day. Apparently Diskare used this place as a way to reward his local bigwig friends. Those in the know could, I was sure, request a private lunch upstairs, one which included some very special services.

I sat silently watching Audrey as Diskare and Simon discussed the weather, the fishing, the market, whatever. The girl refused to acknowledge my gaze and kept her eyes focused on what could be seen of the street from the window next to the table. Iron barred I might add. Finally, she could take it no longer.

"Mr. Wiggins, would you please stop staring at me. It's most disconcerting," she said tersely but politely.

"Pardon me," I said, "I didn't realize I was staring, I'm sorry. It's just that I find you very attractive."

She softened a bit. "Well, I thank you for the complement, and I must apologize for my attitude. I certainly didn't plan on having lunch on this island today. I'm very annoyed. I had hoped to be in the Caymans by dinner." She delivered a stony stare to Simon. He was a slime ball all right.

"Oh, yes Harry, you see it's all my fault," Simon said. Audrey had been talking to me, but the comment was obviously directed at him. "I didn't know", he continued, "that the flight I booked us on stopped here for a layover. We'd been sailing for the last few days, Audrey loves scuba diving, and I guess I just blew it. I'm not very good at travel arrangements and things like that, but it has given me a chance to see my old friend Diskare here."

"You know Simon," the girl's voice was icy and sharp, piercing, "I don't put it past you to have shanghaied me here on purpose just so you could have lunch with one of your drinking buddies. You know I'm really pissed. And you shouldn't get me pissed now, should you?" The girl was flinging daggers at Simon. A silence fell over our little party after the girl's outburst as our waitress appeared to remove our plates. The lunch had been quite delicious, as usual with all of the Club's cuisine, at least as far as staff and guests were concerned. The girl had hardly touched hers, a failure I felt she would soon repent. Slave fare was hardly worth writing home about, that is, assuming that slaves were allowed to write home.

Simon had wolfed down his plateful and was downing his third martini. Diskare, as usual, kept his counsel quietly, observing, measuring. He had a unique skill of talking, but saying little, all the while sizing you up, placing into one of his mind's categories. Filed away for later use.

Diskare acted to break the spell. "Simon, let me show you my new boat, it's very beautiful. Let me take you and Miss Abrams out for a small trip. Our island is actually quite lovely." Diskare looked at Audrey. "Please, let me be your host for a while?" Host, indeed!

"Yes, Audrey let's go see Diskare's boat. We can catch the first flight out in the morning. You don't really want to take that little puddle jumper we booked on do you?" As Simon talked, he waved his arms about like a man agog, knocking over his glass.

"This is it, Simon," the girl said disgustedly as she threw her napkin to the table. "I told you I want off of this island and I meant it. If you don't get ready to go right now, I'm going to go by myself. And remember, in two days, those charge cards you hold will be cancelled. No more flying around the Caribbean for you. I won't have you pissing away my mother's money anymore, my money that is, with your lowlife friends. Now are you going with me or not?"

The girl was quite exercised about the whole thing. I was sure Simon wasn't worth it, but then, I was equally sure that this girl would be apologizing to Simon very shortly.

"I'm staying here with my friends, Audrey," Simon replied. "I'm not going to let you run my life. You'll be sorry you spoke to me like that, I promise you."

Audrey laced out bitterly at Simon. "Well, I'm afraid you're the one who's going to be sorry, Simon. I'm leaving. Mr. Wiggins, would you be so kind as to order me a cab to the airport? I have a plane to catch in one hour. I'm sure that there is some chivalry on even this god forsaken island."

So she was sure, was she? Well, I wouldn't be too hasty. I looked over to Diskare who had been calmly mopping up Simon's overturned martini. He nodded at me discretely. "Harry, the maitre'd will take care of it. Just waive him over." He looked at the girl with his cold steel eyes. "Miss Abrams, I do not appreciate your tone and your implications about me. One should be cautious about making enemies, especially at such a young age." The barracuda was coming out.

"I really don't care what you think, and I don't appreciate being patronized," the girl replied. "I'll wait outside." The maitre'd had come over to the table. "Please call me a cab for the airport at once," she said.

The girl stood and walked away swiftly from the table as the maitre'd scraped and bowed his way to the telephone. Everybody in the now crowded restaurant was watching as they could not have avoided noticing the girl's outburst. Diskare had spoken, as was his custom, firmly, but quietly. Simon was huffing and puffing and waving his arms about as before. I kept my hand on my drink. "Oh well, Simon, we might as well enjoy ourselves, no?" Diskare said.

Diskare motioned the waitress for another round. Easy for him to say, he was drinking seltzer. Maybe I was wrong about what was going on here. How could he just let her walk out? I wasn't getting something. I watched out the window as an island cab, painted about thirty different colors in what seemed to be typical island fashion, drove up to the gate, was admitted and then drove off with the girl in the back seat. Well, I guess I didn't know everything after all.

After another round of drinks, Diskare called for the check and signed it. "Now Simon, you don't really want to go on my boat, do you?" He smiled at Simon.

"Boat? Who wants to go on a fucking boat?" Simon laughed, a kind of greasy guffaw.

"I thought not. May I suggest that you go upstairs and refresh yourself for a while, I'm sure you will find something there which will arouse your interest."

"Oh, I'm sure you're right old buddy, I'm sure you're right."

"And then we will see you, perhaps around nine tonight?"

"You can count on that amigo." Simon was beginning to sound like a very poor caricature of a slimy, fat, good old boy. Well, ducks don't fall far from the tree, do they?

Diskare and I left the restaurant and he directed his limousine back to the club. I was speechless, as I was disturbed at my misreading of the situation. Diskare had a little smile on his face. "Quite a lovely creature, wasn't she, Harry?" he asked as the car sped out onto the mountain roadway leading out of the city.

"Yes, quite lovely, but one that got away, no?"

"Well Harry, sometimes you have to let things take their course, do you know what I mean?"

I nodded yes, and as Diskare's tone seemed to signal an end to the conversation, I dummied up and enjoyed the scenery which quickly flashed past the window as we motored along. About fifteen minutes into our ride, I saw the taxi which had left the restaurant coming down the mountain road in the opposite direction. It was empty except for the driver, and that wasn't the way to the airport. It seemed that our little friend had missed her plane after all. I looked at Diskare.

"You see, Harry, timing is everything. I believe we have a new guest waiting for us at the Club. Shall we return and greet her?"

I really didn't have to say anything, I just nodded and smiled. This would be interesting indeed.

We drove up to the club a short while later and were waived through the front gate. The driver pulled us over to the side door of the main house and we entered by that door. As we walked in, I could see the guards giving the car the once over. Even the top man's car was subject to search when he returned. No telling who would try what, but safety lay in precautions. Needless to say that some people might look askance at Diskare's little operation here. Not only was he guilty of kidnapping, rape, involuntary servitude, piracy and murder, but a substantial amount of contraband found its way in and out of this island. And it also served as a safe little getaway for some of the toughest, baddest bad guys this side of zero meridian. Many a deal meaning only bad news for the guardians of law, order and the good guy way had been struck here.

Passing through the hallway, Diskare led me through the doors to his private office. There, sitting in a large, overstuffed, maroon, leather chair was Audrey. And steaming was an understatement.

"I thought so," she yelled, "I was positive you were behind this. What the fuck do you think you are doing? I have never been treated like this in my life, brought here against my will. This is kidnapping. Let me tell you, I intend to press charges. I don't care if the president of this island is your Uncle Charlie, you are going to pay for this!" The girl was standing now, stamping her foot and jabbing her finger at Diskare. Her eyes bulged slightly from their sockets and her face was turning a sort of soft pink. Very excited.

There was one guard in the room standing about five feet behind the chair the girl had been sitting on. He stood there stony faced, looking only at Diskare. I'm sure he was a little curious at why Diskare would take this kind of shit from a woman, especially one who was a prisoner and soon to be a slave.

The room was finely furnished with a teakwood-topped desk and leather appointed chairs and stools. A heavy mahogany armoire stood against one wall while on the opposite one was a large plate glass window which looked out over the bay below. A red, plush carpet covered the center areas of the floor, leaving a border of gleaming, highly polished wood around the room.

Diskare just walked calmly past the girl to the business end of his desk, ignoring her outburst. His desk was set facing the doors we had entered through and the girl had been sitting in one of two elegant leather easy chairs which faced it, their backs to the door. Beyond the desk, to Diskare's rear, was an array of three chairs, their backs also to the door, all facing a divan set about two feet out from the wall. Diskare motioned me to one of those chairs. He spoke to the girl.

"Let me say this to you one time. I am not Simon. I do not accept verbal abuse from anyone, especially women. I have had you brought here and you are in a very difficult situation." This was barracuda par excellence; he spoke slowly and harshly. "I suggest strongly you shut your mouth and sit over there." He pointed to the divan. "Or the gentleman behind you will make you very sorry."

The girl was startled to hear Diskare take the offensive so quickly. She was also certainly impressed with his tone and perhaps the first inkling that she wasn't in Kansas anymore was creeping into her brain. She was a cool one though and was only momentarily non-plussed. Eying first the guard and then Diskare warily she said, "And I do not take orders from anyone, especially any dirt bag friends of my step father." A good riposte, but here she showed her facade was on shifting sand.

Diskare just stared at her, glaring. The girl wavered, "I'll do as you ask, but I expect a full explanation for my treatment and it better be good."

She walked over to the divan and sat down. I followed her over to the array of chairs and, picking out the one nearest the window, to her right, and sat down. I had a good view of the girl, sitting primly on the divan. It was slightly lower than the chairs and so she had to raise her head to look at me. I noticed for the first time a set of rings which dangled from the sides of the divan, on the corners and in the middle of each side. No doubt what they were for. Diskare sat down in the middle chair directly facing the girl, the guard shifting discretely behind her, about ten feet to her right.

Her chest was heaving with her pent up anger, pressing her breasts out both upwards, slightly out of her neckline and forward towards us. I was speculating idly about the size and color of her nipples. Based on her light complexion I imagined them to be light, almost pink. Her wide, pouty lips promised large, fleshy areolas. I had no doubt that I would soon know for sure.

"Mr. Wiggins, I can't believe you had anything to do with this." The girl was a sharpie all right, strike first, divide and conquer. The ball was in my court.

"Let's just say that I was not in the loop on this one," I rejoined. "But what's done is done." I shrugged my shoulders.

Diskare laughed.

"A true diplomat Harry." And to the girl, "Now, you will calm down and we will have a little chat." At that moment the door to the office opened and Carla walked in followed by a servant girl carrying a tray of glasses and a pitcher of liquid.

"Ah, Carla, you are so thoughtful. Thank you for joining us, and with refreshments." He turned to the girl. "I only drink soft drinks before dark, Miss Abrams. Please join me in a lemonade." Diskare motioned to Carla who poured four glasses from the servant's tray. She handed one each all around and kept one for herself. She sat in the third chair, to Diskare's right. The servant placed the tray on a nearby table and stood aside, her back to the wall, her head down, her wrists crossed before her.

"Now, let me see, how to begin?" Diskare said, sipping at his glass. "You are surprised and alarmed at being brought here. I can hardly blame you for that. I must say that I am not enamored of your disposition, however." The girl piqued.

"Now see here Mr. Diskare, if you believe I'm going to sit here and have you lecture me on my manners after...."

She never finished her sentence. Diskare had motioned to the guard at the beginning of the girl's outburst. The guard, a well-tanned, muscular island fellow, calmly but swiftly stepped over to the girl, grabbed the drink from her with one hand and with the other landed a slap across her face that rattled her teeth and almost knocked her off of the divan. The girl's face turned beet red where she had been slapped. The sound of the slap had been like the crack of a whip and the complete silence which followed it served only to highlight its force.

After a few seconds of disbelief, the girl's hands flew to her face and she began to cry out, "Oh, oh, oh," she began to whine. Diskare's voice lashed out.

"Silence!"

The girl Audrey cut her moan short, staring at Diskare in disbelief. "For the last time," he told her, "you will shut your mouth and be quiet. Do you understand?" Diskare's visage was like iron, his eyes piercing the girl's.

Clearly, the girl's bravado had flown the coop. She nodded hastily, rubbing her face with her hands, tears starting to form in the corners of her eyes. She trembled slightly.

"Now, as I was saying," Diskare continued, "I dislike your attitude. But that is of little moment just now. What is important is to advise you, since, as you have correctly surmised, you are now no longer in control of your own fate, of our intentions with regard to you."

Diskare let the import of his words sink in. The girl was staring at him, one hand still rubbing her face, the other clutching her blouse before her.

"As you made so clear at lunch, in two days you are to come into a great fortune. About thirty million dollars I believe. And by so doing, you would cut off my good friend, and client I might add, Simon Delacourt, your stepfather. We, that is me and the men for whom I work, have decided that we will not let that happen. For a not modest fee, we have acted so that our friend Simon will not be forced to give up the style of life to which he has become accustomed in the ten years since your mother's death. Also, his control of several important companies has proven quite useful and profitable to us. It is important to us to be able to continue to utilize these facilities to conduct our affairs. We have therefore decided to detain you indefinitely so that you cannot take control of this empire."

The implications of this statement were clearly apparent to the girl. Her mouth opened wide in an expression of shock. She looked at Diskare, eyes wide, staring in disbelief. She looked at me and then Carla, as if we would dispel the harshness of the words which were assaulting her ears. "Oh my god" she uttered softly. "Oh, god, this can't be real."

"Oh yes, Miss Abrams, this is very real. You are not flying to the Caymans tonight, or ever." Diskare let the words sink in.

Audrey, forgetting momentarily her slap, took the offensive once again. "You'll never get away with this. Hundreds of people know where I am. Someone will track me down. It's ridiculous, you can't do this."

"Oh yes we can, Miss Abrams, we can very well. You see, we know that hundreds of people know, or will discover, that you were on our little island today. Maybe thousands, eventually. But you see, also many people saw you today leave a crowded restaurant and drive away alone in a taxicab. You were headed for the airport. There will be additional witnesses, let us say, friendly to our cause, who will swear that they saw you board our little island "puddle jumper" as Simon called it. Your suitcase was loaded aboard that plane at your instructions soon after you were deposited here. And there will be ample evidence that that plane took off of this island," Diskare looked at his watch, "about ten minutes ago. In about an hour, it will develop engine trouble. After radioing its position to the authorities, it will go down in the sea. The pilot will be saved. But you, I am sorry to report, you will not be seen again. Your luggage will float to the surface as the final evidence that you were on that flight, but you, at least as far as the world is concerned, will go down with the plane to a watery grave in five thousand feet of water."

The trap had now been sprung. The victim was caught tight in the web. She could struggle, but there was no escape. The magnitude of her predicament struck the girl like a fist. I could almost feel her heart drop as she took in Diskare's words like a prisoner at the bar listening to the sentence of the court: death.

The girl started moaning slightly, rocking back and forth. She had now covered her face with her hands, as if to block out the words that she was hearing, each one a dagger. Diskare calmly sipped his lemonade, his eyes glued to the girl. Carla too had her eyes fastened on the girl. On her face, though, was eagerness, impatience. She was clearly pining to get at this new victim. The guard stood there passively, as if possessed of only a passing interest in the proceedings. He had probably witnessed many girls in this position. Girls who, sooner or later, became available to him. Girls like the slave who stood demurely and quietly, her back against the wall, waiting for an order, knowing her function: serve and obey.

The girl, Audrey, was permitted a few more moments of quiet crying. She murmured softly behind her hands and rocked back and forth on the divan. The three of us sitting before her just watched in silence. Suddenly, from behind her hands she spoke, pleading, frantic, "Oh, please, please don't do this to me! I haven't hurt you! I haven't hurt anyone! I'll give you whatever you want! Please, oh, please." She peered out from behind her hands. "I'm sorry for having insulted you, Mr. Diskare, please don't do this to me, please!"

Diskare just maintained his piercing glare. The girl could see that her pleading was useless. Her face disappeared again behind her hands. "Oh, I can't believe this! It can't be happening! It can't!"

Diskare broke his silence. "Oh, yes my dear, it can and is happening. And as far as giving us whatever we want, well, we have that already. We have you and we have our friendship with your stepfather. All that is really left is what shall we do with you."

The girl looked at Diskare. "What do you mean?"

"Well, there are really only two choices. We cannot let you go under any circumstances. That would just frustrate the whole purpose of having brought you here. We can't just let you pine away in some cell somewhere. That would be a waste and too troublesome for us. So there are, as I have said, only two choices."

"What choices? What are you going to do with me?" The girl was frantic, but trying not to completely give in to her panic, trying to hold on in face of the impossible, the unreal. There was little doubt that she had never imagined herself in a position like this in her whole, young life.

"Well, as I said, there are two choices. The first is easy. Since we cannot have you return to the world outside and interfere with our plans, we could easily eliminate that possibility by causing your death, for real this time. Philippe, show Miss Abrams here the little tool you use for terminations."

The guard grinned widely. Now was his turn to participate in this little drama. Clearly, this was a specialty of his, and one that he enjoyed. He removed from under his shirt a short, thin cord, each end wound around a wooden handle: a quite effective garrote. The girl's eyes blazed with fear as the guard approached her, the garrote fully extended between his arms. Without comment, he slipped it over her head, crossing his arms first, and then pulled it tight. The girl sat upright like she had been struck by lightening. Her hands flew to her neck as she frantically tried to pull the cord away from her throat. The guard just grinned more broadly and pulled the garrote tighter.

"Now, Miss Abrams, as I said, this is choice number one. All you have to do is say the word and I will have Philippe snuff out your life. It will only take a few moments, and we will enjoy the show, believe me." Philippe had pulled the garrote so tight that the girl's face was starting to turn red. She arched her back, trying to move away from the pressure on her neck, her feet pushing off of the floor. She gurgled loudly, her eyes bulging, pleading. It was impossible for her to say anything, and I was sure that Diskare knew that. More games.

"Ah, perhaps you would like to hear about the other choice first? Very well. Philippe, you may release the girl. For now that is." Philippe relaxed the garrote slowly, the girl gasping for breath. As Philippe retreated, I could see a thin red line around her throat. The skin remained unbroken, but the evidence of the tightness of the garrote was there. Apparently Philippe was indeed an expert, being able to produce the tightness required for asphyxiation without breaking the skin. A light touch.

The girl was coughing and crying, not knowing which to do first. The guard, at Diskare's motion, handed back to her the glass of lemonade that he had taken from her before. As he handed it to her, he caught her eye, leering meaningfully. When the glass was empty, he placed the empty back on the small table near the window and resumed his position behind and to the right of the girl, an arm's length away. The girl looked up at Diskare, rubbing her throat. She was near hysteria. "Please don't kill me, please! I'll do whatever you ask, please don't kill me! I don't want to die, please!"

Diskare waited for her to regain some of her composure. "A very appropriate statement considering the nature of the second choice. In fact, exactly what I had in mind." Diskare chuckled menacingly. "I think another demonstration would be the best way to convey the essence of choice number two." He motioned over to the slave girl who had been standing quietly against the wall the entire time. She at once came forward, kneeling in front of Diskare. Diskare stroked her head softly, gazing into her face. He then grabbed her face by the cheeks from under her chin and turned her head towards Audrey.

"A lovely face, no? I think she is exquisite. And well trained too. She has been with us, for how long Carla?"

"About two years, Mr. Diskare." Carla replied.

"Yes, a very exquisite face, and body too. Would you like to see her body Miss Abrams?"

Audrey, still rubbing her neck, but somewhat calmer now, looked confused. "I don't understand."

"Oh you will, Miss Abrams, you will, very shortly." Diskare brought the servant girl's face back to his. "What is your name?" The girl spoke softly, her eyes focused downwards, her hands crossed before her. "I have been given the name Maria, Master," she replied. She was indeed lovely, long, thick black hair, curled into waves which flowed down her back like a mountain cascade. Her waist was narrow, accentuating her broad hips. Her breasts, large and round, were pushed up by the stays beneath the bodice of her dress, the same one worn by all of the house servants. Her nipples were barely visible above the top of the top of her dress. They were taut and flush, their redness contrasting sharply with the creamy whiteness of the fabric. Her skin, brown, like cocoa, her eyes bright and clear.

"Maria, please show Miss Abrams you beautiful breasts, in fact, why don't you remove your dress?"

The servant girl rose from her knees, pausing only long enough to murmur, "Yes, Master."

She pulled the shoulders of her dress down her arms and down to her waist. She was standing to Diskare's right, Audrey's left, and I had a good view of her as her breasts sprang free. They were the same cocoa color as the rest of her skin except for several long, red welts running across her chest. Her pubic area had been shaved and she sported the usual golden ring which all of the girls here were marked with. She folded her dress neatly next to her and stood at attention, her arms crossed before her.

Except for the collar around her neck, the leather bracelets on her wrists and the same around her ankles, she was naked.

Audrey looked on in amazement. I wasn't sure which impressed her more, the fact that this girl had disrobed without hesitation upon Diskare's mere suggestion, the badges of the girl's enslavement or the marks of the whip across her breasts and thighs. But clearly she was impressed.

"A lovely creature, isn't she, Miss Abrams? And her beauty belongs to me and those others of our little club here who desire to possess it. You see, she is a slave, property, chattel. She has been taught to obey and to serve. Maria, stand closer to Miss Abrams, show her the ring in your loins."

The servant girl stepped towards Audrey. Audrey recoiled, but could not tear her gaze away from the glittering metal between Maria's thighs. Maria spread them open and lifted the disk that was there between them so that Audrey could read the inscription. She was no more than three feet away from Audrey's face. I knew what the disk said since it was identical on all of the girl's here. The front was marked only by a scrolled "*k*", set upon a field of crossed whips. The reverse contained the Klitzman motto "serve and obey" written over the girl's name.

"Maria, come and kneel before me." Diskare motioned the servant girl over to him. She knelt in front of him, her knees apart, her wrists set back on her hips. "Forehead to the floor," he commanded. The girl obeyed. Audrey now had a view of the servant girl's backside, also laced with the marks of the whip. Someone had obviously prepared this girl for her role here today, a kind of demonstration model. But what really caught Audrey's attention was the brand. Located on the right cheek of the girl's ass, just below her hip, was the sign of her enslavement, a large, red, cursive "*k*", burned deep into the servant girl's flesh.

"You see Miss Abrams, this is the second choice. You may choose to be enslaved. Of course if you do, you will cease to have any identity other than as a piece of property. You may be used, or abused, at will by me, Mr. Wiggins here, Carla, the guard or any one of the members or guests of our club who desire you. Like this little creature here," Diskare lifted the head of the servant girl, forcing open her mouth with his fingers, "you will be marked and then taught to serve and obey. Carla, why don't you pick out a nice collar and some whips for Miss Abrams to examine. That might help her make her decision."

Carla rose from her chair and walked to the armoire. She opened it with a small key and drew from it a leather collar together with a whip and a riding crop. She then placed them on the floor before Audrey. In the meantime, Diskare had drawn the servant girl Maria from her knees and had tumbled her across his lap. His hand probed her loins. The girl gave a little gasp as he thrust his fingers inside her. None of this was lost on Audrey. She flashed her eyes back and forth between Carla, the display that now lay before her and the spectacle of the violation of the slave girl. Then, for a moment, she froze, her hands clasped before her as if in prayer. She then bent over and began sobbing heavily.

I must say that Diskare was really playing this for all that it was worth. A nice touch too, letting the girl choose. She would feel her bonds even more severely knowing that it was her own act which enslaved her. On the other hand, maybe he was playing his hand too strongly. Was slavery really a fate worse than death? We would shortly know.

Diskare motioned for the guard to step closer to Audrey. The guard dangled the garrote from his hands. "And now, Miss Abrams, you must choose death or slavery. What is your choice?"

Audrey looked up from her lap, "Oh, please don't do this. I've never hurt anyone. Why are you doing this? Please, please, don't hurt..."

In the middle of her pleas Philippe passed the garrote once more around her throat. He pulled it tight with a smooth jerk, forcing Audrey's head back, deftly avoiding her hands.

Audrey's eyes popped out as she grasped vainly at the cord of the garrote now around her neck. Her feet flayed wildly she tried to arch her back to reduce the pressure on her neck. Philippe pulled tighter for a moment and then relaxed slightly, causing the girl to sit back on the divan, her feet to the floor. She looked at Diskare in horror.

"Now, my child, you must choose. If you fail to choose, I will permit Philippe to choose for you. And he has never failed to choose death. So now speak, what do you choose?"

Audrey face was contorted with fear and despair. I could see that she was too frightened even to speak. Her lips moved but no sound came out. Her face was turning red.

"Silence?" Diskare spoke to the quivering girl seated before him, his hand still buried in the other girl's sex. He signaled to Philippe, "Then kill her."

Philippe paused for a moment, gathering himself to pull the ends of the garrote apart, to tighten the noose around the girl's throat. In just that instant, the girl found her voice. She screamed out, her voice strained by the cord around her throat, her face frantic. "Oh my god, no, please don't kill me! I don't want to die! I'll do anything, anything! I'll be your slave, anything, just please don't kill, please!" Philippe continued his pause and looked at Diskare. Diskare smiled and motioned for him to loosen the garrote.

"Ah, you have chosen. Good. Philippe, you may release her."

Philippe, appearing somewhat disappointed, backed off from Audrey and removed the garrote once again. Audrey emerged, coughing and sputtering for breath. Her eyes were red and her face puffed up from crying. Tears cascaded down her face as she sat and sobbed in relief. She wasn't given long to rejoice. "Miss Abrams, you will kneel before me. Now!" Diskare's voice boomed like a cannon shot at the girl. She stiffened as if shot and then fell to her knees in front of Diskare, her dress spread out like the petals of a flower around her.

"Kneel up straight. Arms at your side." The girl complied. Diskare pushed Maria off of his lap and to his side towards Carla. He edged forward on his chair and stared Audrey in the face, inches away. Between them on the floor lay the riding crop and whip and the collar Carla had removed from the armoire a short while ago.

"You will now beg to be a slave! Beg, or Philippe will finish the job he started!"

Audrey hesitated briefly, and then whispered quietly, her voice cracked with fear and sorrow, "Please let me be a slave. Please let me live. I want to live, please." The tears continued to flow.

"You must beg, Miss Abrams. You must beg to be a slave. Now, or die." Diskare grabbed the girl's cheeks between his right hand.

"I beg to be a slave. Please let me live. I beg you, please let me be a slave," she whined disconsolately

Diskare smiled. The barracuda had his kill. "Harry, should we let this girl become a slave? What do you think?"

"Well," I replied, "why don't you try her out? If she doesn't work out you can always kill her later. No?"

"I think you're right, Harry. Don't you Carla?"

"I think that's a splendid idea Mr. Diskare. In fact, I believe that she will be a very good slave. She's quite attractive and she has such a strong will to live. I think she'll train very well." The expert was talking.

"Then it's settled." Diskare squeezed the girl's face harder and glared into her face, his voice like a whip. "I accept you as a slave. As of this moment your body is not your body, your will is not your will. Your life is only borrowed from us, your masters. From this moment on you will obey and you will serve. Your hands, your breasts, your loins, they exist only to please those who own you and command you. Serve and obey, these are the words you must forge into your brain. You will do so silently and with relish. Any failure on your part to please, any hesitancy in obeying a command, no matter how painful or distasteful will be punished severely. Since your life is now ours, it is ours to end. Remember that. Do you understand?"

The girl nodded her head, still held in Diskare's hand. "Good. Now let's see what our new property looks like. You will stand and strip. First remove your blouse."

Audrey jumped to her feet and began to unbutton her blouse. Her hands, however, were too shaky from her recent dance with Philippe to do the job. She looked in horror at Diskare as she fumbled.

"Not a very good beginning, slave. Perhaps Maria should help you. Maria, strip this slave."

Maria, who had been kneeling next to Carla, sprung to her feet and quickly unbuttoned Audrey's blouse. Beneath it, her breasts were wrapped in a thin, lace bra which pushed the breasts up. Audrey had dropped her hands to her sides and Maria was able to reach around Audrey's back and disconnect the strap.

For an instant, the two women stood front to front, Maria's naked breasts crushed against Audrey's. Then Maria slid the straps down Audrey's arms and pulled off the bra. She must have known her business since she then stepped away, behind Audrey, permitting us a free view of her breasts. I had been right. Her nipples and aureoles were pale, only slightly darker than her pale, white skin. Pale, but large and fleshy, like half dollars. Her nipples were hard, stiffened by fear. The breasts themselves were slightly more pale than her skin, showing the effects of years of bikini sunbathing. Well those tan marks would be gone soon. A bikini was considered overdressing around here.

Diskare paused only to take in the sight of his new property. He was appraising her, the game over, the real stuff now to begin. Should he ship her off the Klitzman's? Would she serve well here? Maybe a sale to a South American drug king? Well there was time for decisions like that later. First she would be trained and marked. She would taste the lash, have men enter her body at will, suffer hours or even days of painful confinement. She would learn to service women as well, both for the pleasure of the few queens of crime who favored this little resort and for Carla, a demanding mistress. From time to time, she would perform for her masters, pleasuring anther slave, or being pleasured for the delight of those who favored that taste. Her mouth would open to receive the members of those who deigned to possess it, licking and sucking with new found skill, a skill she would develop quickly or she would feel the painful consequences of failure. Perhaps she would be taught to dance, to flaunt her charms before those with the power to accept her invitations, unwilling as they may be. I was looking forward to it.

Diskare motioned the girl to continue with her undressing. With a sob she unfastened the buttons of her skirt and let it fall to the floor. She stood before us in her panties, her light brown pubis peeking through the sides of her crotch. Her mound was full, presenting a slight but noticeable bulge above the vee of her legs. She was shaking.

"The rest!" Diskare ordered. The girl looked up at him briefly and then around the room. The slave Maria stood there stoically awaiting a command. Carla sipped her drink and stared back at Audrey. I was entranced and more than excited as the bulge in my pants revealed. Audrey hooked her thumbs into the sides of her panties and pulled them down, stepping out of them and casting them aside.

"There will be a punishment later for your slowness in obeying my commands. Do not err again." Diskare's voice was as cold as ice. The girl was sobbing.

"Now lay down on the divan behind you, face up and spread your arms and legs." Audrey jumped to obey, tears flowing down her cheeks. Diskare motioned to Phillipe who stepped forward.

"Phillipe, please place the bracelets and collar on my new slave." Phillipe needed no second urging. He stepped forward and collected the instruments of Audrey's possession from the floor. Leaning over her body, kneeling between her legs, he first affixed the collar. It locked closed with a snap. The ankle bracelets were next and then, one by one, the wrists.

"Now, slave, stand up and present yourself to your new masters." Diskare ordered.

Audrey sat up, her hands flying to her throat, her eyes staring, non-believing, at her leather cuffs. Remembering Diskare's imprecations about obedience and pain, she leapt to her feet and rushed to stand before him. "W,what will happen now?" she managed to squeak out in a tiny voice, a stark contrast to her stern rapprochements of a few minutes before.

"Slaves don't act questions." Diskare replied. "A second punishment."

Audrey squealed slightly as she realized her error. Oh, well, trial and error is sometimes the best teachers.

"Maria, clip this slave's wrists to the back of her collar." Maria moved to obey instantly. When she had finished, Audrey stood before us, her chest jutted out, her breasts raised up invitingly, her arms behind her head.

"Carla, I would like you to take this slave to the punishment room and administer ten lashes with a riding crop, front and back. She is then to be gagged and confined until this evening when we will have her marked. Mr. Delacourt will be here about nine o'clock. I'm sure he will enjoy the event. I would like to give him the pleasure of fucking her first so make sure that no one has access to her until then. Maria, Phillipe has worked hard for us today. Escort him to your chamber and please him." Maria nodded submissively. Phillip grinned.

Carla was grinning too. She stepped forward and attached a leash to Audrey's collar. Audrey flinched when she approached but offered no resistance. She could sense that Carla was one to be feared.

"By the way slave," Diskare remarked to the girl as she was being led away, "I have not decided on your new name yet. For now you will continue to answer to the name Audrey as I think it will amuse Mr. Delacourt. Tomorrow we may think of a new name for you. Harry, I'm feeling quite randy after this little episode. Let's go down to the training rooms and select a little delight for ourselves."

"My pleasure, Mr. Diskare.," I responded, "my pleasure." I finished my lemonade as the new slave, temporarily called Audrey, was led swiftly from the room.

## PART TWO
## HARRY IN NEW YORK/MARA'S STORY

## CHAPTER ONE
## HARRY LEARNS THE ROPES

I was sitting in the tiny kitchen of an Upper East Side New York City apartment, waiting as had been planned. I had gained entry easily with a key that had been made from a wax impression by one of Draco's people. It was a modern type apartment, clean, new rugs, stark, bright designs. The kind of place that money slept in. I had been there since about 9 p.m., biding my time, listening, waiting.

I had spent a little over a week at Diskare's resort. The beach had been pleasant, the women sublime. Audrey's initiation into slavery was a memorable event. Diskare let Simon press the hot brand into her buttocks, completing her formal loss of human rights. She had begged and pleaded with him frantically not to do it, to set her free. She promised him everything she could think of, including signing over her deceased mother's financial empire to him. Simon didn't budge an inch or blink an eye. When he fucked her for the first time, I could see the pure enjoyment he got out of it and the wave of relief as his problem of what to do about her assuming control of the family companies withered away. I didn't fuck Audrey that night, but I did have her suck me off the night before I left for the States. She wasn't bad.

Shortly after midnight, I heard a key in the lock. It was the girl. The lights came on in the room just as I slipped myself into the walk-in pantry closet. I could hear her high heels clicking loudly on the parquet floor of the kitchen. She must have walked right past me. I was ready to make my move if she opened the door, but she didn't and I listened to her footsteps click away and become silent as she stepped onto the carpet in the living area. I opened the closet door slowly. The lights of the kitchen had been turned out and I could see the lights of the bedroom down the hallway. I stepped quietly from my hiding place and walked slowly towards the bedroom.

I felt in my pocket for the knockout agent Draco had given me and the cloth with which to cover her mouth. It was there and ready. The same motion which would suffice to bring out the cloth would release the agent as I squeezed down hard on the plastic ball inside with my gloved right hand. Whatever else I needed was in the small carrying case in my other hand. "Planning, caution, execution." Those were Draco's words. Well the first part was over. The second was here, the third, coming up.

I could hear the girl humming softly to herself in her bedroom as, presumably, she was undressing for bed. In a minute or two I would be able to hear the water running in the bathroom which would signal my entry into the bedroom. I knew the layout of the apartment well and knew that even if the bathroom door was open, she would not be able to see me as I entered the bedroom and took up my position. After a short while, I heard the water begin to run. She was washing her face, taking off her makeup. The next time she put it on would be for someone else's benefit, and certainly not without the approval of those who she was destined to serve. Her life was about to change.

"Know your prey." That was Draco's other pet phrase. Draco and I had picked out our prey after a week of careful stalking. We had had several leads from spotters who Draco kept on his payroll, but this one had panned out the best. She was young and beautiful. That went without saying. She would not have been brought to our attention otherwise. She lived alone and kept regular hours. Her building had an emergency staircase which led directly to the street. For the last three nights we had monitored her movements as she came home from work.

Each night she would come home, eat dinner, watch the news and go back out. Every night she returned about midnight after attending her classes at City College and studying in the school library. This revealed enough about her to make Draco decide to pounce. Most importantly, however, Draco's data check had not revealed anything particularly important about her. She was just another 22 year old going to college at night for her MBA, and working during the days as an assistant market analyst for a national corporation. Just the type that made our country great, hard worker, clean liver, dull, dull, dull. Well, after tonight her life wouldn't be dull, not at all.

I thought briefly about the things which were undoubtedly going to happen to this girl. A pang of guilt, yes. A loss of resolve, no. I had decided, weeks ago that whatever I had to do to bring down Klitzman, I would do. More than just the fate of some yuppie fortune builder was at stake. She was just a casualty in a war. A civilian casualty, sure, but since when did being a civilian exempt anyone from suffering in war. Not since Cain slew Able.

Quickly but quietly I made my way into the bedroom. I could hear her splashing herself at the sink, still humming. What was that song, I couldn't make it out. An older tune, I should know it. As I heard her begin to brush her teeth, I positioned myself next to the doorway. I stayed far enough back that it would take her a step or two into the room to see me, even if she were looking, but close enough to grab her as soon as she passed over the threshold. I looked carefully round the room. I made sure that my reflection could not be seen as she came through the door. Her dress was laid carefully across the bed, her shoes together. Neat as a pin. She would probably have made a good executive, but would make a better slave.

I knew her habits pretty much. Home at 12, then a little TV; in bed before lights out. I had listened to the bugs we had placed to find out what we could about her movements. I had spent about an hour that night removing them so that they wouldn't be here for anyone to find when her disappearance was noted. I had also packed a small bag of her clothes and typed a message on her computer to the effect that she had decided to take a few days off. A "friend" would call her in sick to her job in the morning. The day after being Saturday, and Monday a holiday, she wouldn't be missed until Tuesday or even Wednesday. By then she could be out of the country.

Suddenly, the teeth brushing stopped and she turned off the water. I poised, waiting. She turned off the bathroom light and seconds later, walked through the door. As she passed me she was pulling off her chemise, her eyes covered, blinded. I stepped softly behind her, waiting for her to take the lacy undergarment off of her head. As I leapt towards her, she caught a glimpse of me out of the corner of her eye. Too late.

Grabbing the cloth in my right hand, I squeezed hard, flushing it with the knockout agent which had been stored in the plastic container. With my left arm I reached across her chest and pulled her towards me. I brought my right hand down across her face at the same time. I heard her gasp in surprise. A textbook reaction, and one which would guarantee the success of the chemical. I felt her move her arm upwards in preparation for a downwards jab. Someone had taught this girl some self defense. By the time she was ready to bring it down, though, she was out and collapsed in my arms.

I held the cloth to her mouth for another few seconds to make sure and then dragged her body over to the bed. I let her down softly and pulled out a plastic bag from my pocket into which I jammed the cloth I had used. No use getting all fucked up on the fumes myself. I went to the window and pulled the blinds open and shut twice. My signal. I had made sure when I came in that the blinds were shut. No need for any 'Rear Window' heroes to call the cops.

I regarded the girl on the bed. She was thin, shapely, her hair was a strawberry blond, short, in a flip. Her legs were long and firm, the kind that felt good wrapped around your back. I knew from our background check that she worked out at the local health club. One of Draco's people, a woman, had been able to gain access to the club the night the girl was there. The pictures she took in the locker room helped seal this girl's fate. Draco didn't really appreciate going to the trouble of acquiring a girl unless he was sure it was worthwhile. The pictures had proven that, demonstrating her firm muscles, energetic body and pure, unblemished skin. All that working out would pay off all right, but not for her.

I moved quickly since the knockout agent would keep her under for only a few minutes. She was wearing only her panties and bra. They were white, cotton, plain but pretty. I reached into my pocket and pulled out two lengths of cord. I took her hands, tied them behind her back and then crossed her ankles and tied them together too. I lifted her up and pulled her farther up on the bed so that she was stretched out its full length on her back. She started coming around. I took the gag from my little bag of tricks and filled her mouth with it, fastening its two ends behind her head. As I finished, she started to stir and her eyes popped open. She saw me above her and made as if to get up off the bed and run. Only then did she realize that she was bound hand and foot. Her eyes played frantically around the room and then focused on me.

I leaned over the bed and brought my face inches away from hers. My hand was on her throat. "You will not be hurt if you do not struggle." I told her in a low voice. "If you do, I will have to hurt you, do you understand?"

She nodded yes frantically. Her eyes were as wide as silver dollars. I couldn't blame her. It wasn't everyday that you woke up bound and gagged in your own bedroom. I walked over and turned on the TV. The neighbors must hear everything as usual. I would turn it off in a half hour or so. I then turned out the light and pulled a chair over to the head of the bed and sat down.

The time was exactly 12:15. Draco had said that the pick up would be made at exactly 3 a.m. This was the time when the streets were their emptiest. Most of the night birds had already gone home and the early birds, for the most part, wouldn't be arousing themselves for another hour or so. I would wait. So would the girl.

I had been in the States for about ten days with Draco. We had flown into a small Midwestern city and had leisurely driven across the country to New York. I was nervous as hell coming into the States with a life sentence facing me and all, but the false papers Diskare had given me did the job fine.

We had stopped overnight in Columbus and Pittsburgh to allow Draco to make contact with some of his people. I was with him constantly, or with one of his people, babysitting me. I could see that Draco was being extremely careful. He had his instructions to break me in to the methods of obtaining recruits for Klitzman's empire, and he would do what he was told. But that didn't mean that he couldn't mistrust me. This was one careful dude.

We had taken a room at a midtown businessman's hotel, sharing accommodations. After dinner, we left the hotel and took a taxi uptown to 110th Street and then, after walking a few blocks, making sure we were not followed, grabbed another which took us across the river into the Bronx. We were let out on a deserted corner and then walked a few blocks, checking carefully that we had not been followed.

We stopped in front of a large warehouse building. Draco walked up to a door and knocked twice. A head peeked out of a small window in the door and then it opened. Draco ushered me in. We were met by a slight, Hispanic looking guy, dressed casually but neat. No flashy dressers in Draco's organization. No need to attract unnecessary attention to your self. Just look normal, be normal. This was business and Draco's people were professionals. Besides, Draco's orders were backed up by the fear and respect which Klitzman had earned. No one would make it into this organization if they were a fuck up and nobody would stay alive long if they did.

We went up a short stairway and entered an office on the second floor landing. The room we entered had a large desk surrounded by a few steel chairs, an overhead fluorescent light which flickered slightly. The room was dim, but bright enough for me to see that there was no phone, no filing cabinet, no secretary's area. This was definitely a stripped down operation.

"Florez, this is Harry. He's working with me on this trip," Draco said to the Hispanic. "Let's get to work."

"Sure Mr. Draco," Florez replied. There were two other people in the room, a heavy set white guy, about thirty five, black hair, a face like an ape's, mean and ugly. The other was a woman, about forty, good looking, nice dresser, a bit on the hefty side. After almost two weeks on the road with nothing but Draco for companionship, she looked very good indeed. But we weren't there to socialize.

Draco spoke to the other two. "This here is Harry. He's going to be our inside man. He's done good work and he can handle himself pretty good. Harry, Florez you've met, he's our driver. This here is Sherney, he's the muscle man. And this fine looking lady is Estelle. She's our sitter. Now let's get to work. Estelle, what have you got worked up?"

Estelle spoke softly. "I got us a place in Jersey, about an hour and a half from the GW Bridge. Quiet kind of place, two car garage, full basement, upstairs bedrooms. Nearest neighbor about a half mile away."

"Good, sounds like it'll do fine. Florez, how's our wheels."

"Oh man, I got this great little Econoline. I've built in cabinets on each side for transport purposes, looks just like tool boxes. I got the engine tuned up great. It's real quiet man, like a cat she purrs."

"Okay," Draco said, "Sherney, I know you're ready. Just keep yourself out of any trouble for the next week or two, okay?"

"Sure Draco, no problem."

"All right, I've got a couple of prospects lined up. My primary is this girl on 81st and Broadway. We're going to be staking her out for the next three days. Today's Sunday, if all goes well we'll move on Thursday night. You'll be ready Estelle?"

"I'm ready now, all set up."

"Good. We'll meet here Thursday morning at 11. I'll give you the word then. Florez, you work out a transport route with Estelle. See you all Thursday."

Now, a little over a week later, I was sitting in the dark, biding time. Florez would be gassing up his van and Estelle would be getting ready to receive a visitor. Sherney would ride with Florez. The girl was of course unaware of what the night held for her. She was sitting up against the end of the bed, alert, watching every move I made. I had turned off the TV in accordance with her habits now and opened the blinds. This gave off just enough light for me to see the girl and to make out the rest of the room. There was no need for me to explore anything since I had been in the apartment hours earlier and had done whatever exploring I needed to do then.

On Draco's instructions I had put the girl's jewelry in my bag together with her passport and a couple of bank books. On Friday morning, someone would see to it that the accounts were emptied out. Draco was paid well for his troubles in "recruiting" for Klitzman, but his organization took a lot of grease to keep it going and every little bit helped. Besides, the jewelry and bankbooks were nothing to sneeze at. I'd put the value of the jewelry at about fifteen to twenty thousand. There was double that in the bank accounts. Somebody would figure out a way to get that money out.

There was not much to do now except wait. The girl cried for a long time. Her eyes were pitiful but beautiful. Once in a while, her crying would dissolve into sobs and her ample chest rose and fell deliciously. I resisted my urge to sample her flesh. It had been quite a few days since I had gotten laid and so I was right on the edge. After getting serviced three or four times a day for almost a year, it was like going through withdrawal.

At about 2:30 I decided it was time to get ready. I got up from the chair and leaned over on the bed. The girl jumped as I moved, expecting the worse. She must have thought it pretty weird to be all trussed up like that, a strange man sitting in her bedroom, just sitting there, silently watching her. For two hours? Well, unfortunately for her, she didn't even know what the worse was. It was no problem for me. In prison, you do a lot of waiting.

I spoke to the girl softly. "I am going to untie your feet. You will get up from the bed and come with me to the living room. If you struggle or refuse to cooperate, I will hurt you, and then you will do as I say anyway. Do you understand?"

The girl nodded nervously. I dragged her by her legs down to a lying position and then flipped her over to her stomach. This would make it harder for her to strike out at

me with her feet when I undid the ankle tie. I remembered
the chop she tried to give me when I first grabbed her. After
untying her ankles, still holding one, I pulled her to the edge
of the bed and helped her to her feet by her arm. I stood
behind her, grabbing her hair and pushing her in front of me.
With the other hand I made sure that her wrists were still
tied together. They were.

I led her into the middle of the living room and then
forced her to the floor, face down. Once there I retied her
ankles, and taking a black hood from my pocket, pulled it
over her head and drew it closed around her neck. "You will
remain perfectly still," I whispered into her ear. I don't think
there was much need to tell her that. Bound, hooded, lying
on the floor. A wild man lurking about the apartment. Not
many other choices really.

I went back to the bedroom and got my little bag of tricks
and the bag I had packed with her things. A few seconds
later I was back in the living room. The moonlight shone
through the large living room picture window leaving a
square of light on the rug. It fell across the girl's body
reflecting brightly off of her white underclothes and causing
light shadows which emphasized the curves of her hips, her
thighs. I walked over to her supine form and rolled her over
for a moment onto her back. I could feel her shaking with
fear and could hear her moaning softly behind the gag. All
night she had sat there stoically, awaiting her fate. She had
made no attempt to speak to me, figuring I guess that she
would get her chance. Now it must have been clear to her
that, whatever my purpose was, it didn't include discussing
terms or negotiating with her.

I took in the swell of her breasts as they heaved up and
down in the girl's panic. I placed my hand on the curve of her
hip and then pulled it slowly across the lower part of her
stomach. Soon enough, she would be naked, ready to serve,

but not now. My instructions were clear on that. The girl would remain easier to handle as long as she believed that everything was going to turn out all right. Raping her would tend to convince her that she had nothing to lose by trying to escape, scream for help, run away.

But being so close to the pretty, young woman's pulchritude was too tempting to forgo completely a sampling of her desirous flesh. Her fluffy breasts moved gracefully on her chest as she squirmed beneath me. It was a simple thing to do to slip the strap of her lacy, white bra off her shoulder and allow the cup of her right breast to release her plump orb.

Her dark, expansive areola stared back at me invitingly. The tip of her breast was stiff with fear. The nipple was short and squat with pretty little bumps surrounding it. I seized the breast with my hand appreciatively. It was soft and smooth, as expected, and its warmth stoked my passion. I leaned over and took the bud at her breast's round end in my mouth and sucked it. The girl moaned with displeasure and tried to wriggle free of my grasp. I let my mouth and tongue consume her hard teat while my cock grew and hardened. In a matter of days, perhaps a week, two at most, this modern, independent, free woman would be begging for mercy at the wrong end of a whip. She would happily consume the spunk of anyone who would forestall further torment. I imagined her plush lips encircling my tool, suckling it, much like I was suckling her breast's hard nubbin now.

I pulled myself from my reverie and replaced the breast in its white casement. Regretfully, I rolled the girl back onto her stomach and pulled a hypodermic out of my bag. It contained a knockout drug more powerful than the one I had administered earlier. The idea here was not only to keep her quiet during transportation, but also, to prevent her from having any idea where she was being held. I pulled down her panties, stuck the needle into her rear flesh and gave her the shot before she could react. Her body stiffened at first and then slowly relaxed as the drug started to hit her system. I waited about five minutes until I was sure she was really out and then removed her gag. It wouldn't be nice to have her choke on her own vomit during the trip to New Jersey. You could never tell with these drugs.

I took a long look at the delicate features of her face. Her unconscious face was at rest, devoid of any pretense. Her eyes were shut, of course, her lips parted slightly. Her breathing now relaxed and steady. I took a long, cloth body bag from my smaller bag, unrolled it and opened its top. I rolled the girl over onto her back and then her stomach again, this last roll placing her on top of the bag. I then stuffed her in, first her feet, then her torso and head. I zipped the bag shut.

The time was now 2:55. I dragged the bag over towards the door and brought over my small bag and the suitcase. Recalling Draco's instructions, I went over and took her pocketbook and threw it into my bag. That would've been a mistake. What self respecting young New York woman goes anywhere without her handbag. I also stepped quickly back to the bathroom and put in my bag her makeup kit, her toothbrush and a couple of other things I thought she would take on a trip. I went back to the door and waited.

At 2:59 there was a slight tapping on the door. I checked through the peephole, it was Sherney. He had quietly climbed up the emergency staircase and was ready to help me with my burden down. I let him in and handed him the suitcase. I grabbed the back end of the body bag and he grabbed the front as we stepped quietly out of the apartment. He paused while I put down my end so that I could relock the door.

The emergency door was propped open and we slipped into the staircase. Closing the door behind me, we walked quickly down the five flights of stairs to the ground level.

Sherney, not being as dumb as he looked, had shorted the alarm system for the emergency exit the day before. No one would bother to check it until the girl had been listed missing for a week or two and the authorities began to list her case as suspicious. By then, we would be gone and the police would just have another mystery on their hands.

When we reached the ground floor, Sherney knocked twice quietly on the door. Florez was waiting outside and knocked back twice softly to indicate that the coast was clear. We swiftly hustled our bundles to the van as Florez opened the rear door and climbed in. He pulled on the body bag as Sherney handed him his end. As the bag was swallowed up by the van, I handed Sherney my end and watched him climb in. I glimpsed them placing the bag in the tool locker on the side as I quietly shut the door. In a second, they were off. I walked briskly down the street in the opposite direction where Draco was waiting in his car. I got in and he pulled away from the curb. Florez and Sherney were taking the girl to New Jersey. Draco and I would go back to our hotel. A night's work well done.

## CHAPTER TWO
## MARA'S TALE: MARA MEETS NICKY

I can't really say why I did it. I was in love, yes, but I wasn't a fool. I had been in love before, or what substituted for it. I had gazed into loving eyes gazing back at mine, had felt that terrible longing that separation brought, had felt the angst of love's demise, the loneliness of lost illusions. I had been around. At 27 years old, I thought that schoolgirl crushes were behind me. I had a good job, I was making good money. I had been places, vacations, work trips, school. I knew better, sure. But I did it anyway.

I met Nikos on one of those silly cruises around Manhattan. I had gone on a whim one afternoon when the phone calls, clients and the general mayhem of corporate life had driven me out of the office. The air was just warm enough to be a burden and the idea of a cool, stiff breeze over the water seemed tantalizing. Two hours of total freedom from the pressures of being a wonder woman in New York.

The boat pulled away from the dock and I was standing by the forward railing for about fifteen minutes when I sensed a presence. I looked up saw this tall, dark haired stranger, staring at me. He eyes were warm and humorous, his jaw strong, shoulders broad. I paused a moment before looking away again, my eyes momentarily captured by the allure in his.

Alone for several months, I had broken up with my last boyfriend out of sheer frustration. It was the last in a line of failed relationships with men, boys, really, too interested in themselves to have any interest in anyone else. It wasn't that I didn't get offers. I considered myself as moderately attractive, with thick, shoulder length, chestnut colored hair, a nice figure. My self examination at my mirror each morning before I dressed, showed me breasts that more then filled my hands, a taut, flat belly, and pleasant features with no obvious deformity. Like most women, I was highly critical of my body and I always thought my hips a little too broad, my nose a little too big. I kept my pussy hair well trimmed, regularly painted my fingernails and toes and wore moderate makeup with just a little blush to make up for my somewhat pale skin.

I had decided that I would no longer permit myself to engage in these borderline relationships, had cheered at my last football game, tortured my ears at my last heavy metal/punk/grunge concert, had put up with my last groping, fumbling quick shooter, beer on his breath and stains on his shorts. I would wait, nurture myself, avoid fools and boys, and if any prospective male companion wasn't right, well, I was young, educated, interesting. I could enjoy my own company for a while. I had lived in the city for about two years and I knew a few people, people who were just friends. I didn't need a lover, not at the expense of my personal tastes and standards. That's what I thought.

Two hours later I was stepping off the boat onto the dock with my arm around Nikos', laughing, and, unknowingly, walking into a dark, demonic place in my own soul. We made love that night, his place, and again the next night at mine. I had never had a lover like him, my body on fire as he caressed my breasts and my loins. His touch seemed to light a passion in me like I had never known. After a week or so of this, I couldn't think of anything else. At work, I buzzed through my assignments, finishing in hours what before had taken me days. My boss was ecstatic, not knowing that my sole motivation was to end the day and to drink my fill of Nikos' physical love.

It is easy now to see the progression in our relationship which led me to my demise. At first, I tried to keep some distance. On my way to work I would insist to myself that I would make some excuse, my hair, a girlfriend, work, and take a night off from the physical and emotional frenzy Nikos brewed in me. By lunch time, my resolve would have dissipated and I would be wondering why he hadn't called, where he was, what he was doing. Did he love me? Really? Would he call? Why hadn't he called yet?

Lunch would be like a wasteland, nibbling at my sandwich or salad, literally trembling as I brought hand to mouth. After lunch I would dive into my work, confirmed that all was over that nothing was happening between us. Finally, a call, his voice, delirium.

My need for Nikos, as he called himself, began to dominate my life.

I would come home, nervously opening the door, my heart pounding as the wait for his arrival began. When he did come, sometimes while I was still taking the keys from the door, I would almost faint with anticipation. A kiss hello, a caress, and I was off to the races. More often than not he would take me right there and then, pushing up my skirt, piling me pell mell over the settee, plowing me, his tongue down my throat, his arms pinning me down, imprisoning me in his embrace. I would be on fire as wave after wave of pleasure coursed through me. He would take me slowly, rhythmically, even to his climax, controlling his physical self, while I, ratcheted higher with each thrust, fought wildly to draw him deeper inside me, to have him penetrate my very soul.

I didn't realize it, but it was my soul, my very essence, which he was pursuing and which I was rapidly surrendering to him. After a few weeks, we stopped going anywhere at all. I gave him a copy of my key so that he could wait for me at his leisure or, if he decided to come very late, he could admit himself and surprise me in my bed. He never stayed the night.

After greeting me after work with, if not a fuck, then bringing me to climax with his mouth or his hand, he would slowly strip me, kissing each part of me as the clothes were peeled away. I would remain naked through-out the evening, through dinner, through the cleanup, through coffee and dessert. And then, in the bed-room, an hour, maybe two, caressing, kissing, lovemaking. I would suck him gently, lovingly, each touch of my tongue on his cock an electric jolt to my mind. While I circled his manhood with my lips, he would speak gently, soothingly, urging me on, admiring my body, pulling and pinching my nipples, delicately at first, then harder and then harder still, until I could no longer restrain a moan, both of pain and passion, a moan stifled only by the presence of his swollen, pulsating member in my mouth.

It did not seem odd to me that Nikos spoke so little about himself or his life. Or maybe it did seem odd, but I just didn't care. The apartment where we had gone the first night turned out not to be his own, but borrowed. He had no fixed place of employment, and was mostly unavailable when he was not with me. I didn't question his need to go out many nights after our lovemaking or think necessary to ask him where he spent those nights. I was frankly intrigued by the hints of the illicit in our love. I would fantasize his involvement in a myriad of underworld schemes, his political subversiveness or maybe some darker, evil scheme.

More than once he told me that he would be away for a couple of days. He would miss me he said (I believed him), he would be back soon (I desperately needed to believe him) and he told me he would call. By then I was locked into him irretrievably and I didn't think it strange that he insisted that I maintain as best I could our routine and customs (as he called them) to remain naked, alone, while I awaited his return, dressing only to go to work and come home. I was to maintain my sexual activity, by myself, according to instructions given by him, caressing myself before my bedroom mirror, legs akimbo, thinking of him.

And think of him I did. At the appointed hour I placed the chair before the mirror on the inside of the bedroom door, and stroked myself, first my breasts, my stomach my thighs and then my loins, bringing myself to climax, with his name on my lips.

Nor did it seem unusual when, one evening, he brought out video and still cameras and had me pose, legs spread, bent over, breasts pushed up and offered to the camera. I undressed for the video, slowly, sensuously, and then, as I had before him on many occasions, and had done alone, on his instructions, caressed myself until shuddering and crying out I came, shamelessly, without reservation.

I did anything he asked or demanded. Several times I met him at downtown hotels, an hour's workout, then back to work. Once he called me during the middle of the afternoon and instructed me to go to the ladies room and bring myself off. I was shocked, fearful. Not only was this an intrusion into my last sanctuary from my relentless need for him, but what would someone think, coming into the john to hear me panting and moaning behind the swinging door of a stall? But I did it. I did it because, well, I don't know why other than the fact that his demand made me want to. To satisfy him, yes, but more. I needed to ensure that other demands, a continuous stream of them would be given to me, proof of his wanting, needing me, the more the better. I had given myself over totally to my need of him. Or so I thought. Events were to prove that I had one more thing to give.

## CHAPTER THREE
## HARRY GETS AN AU PAIR

A few nights later, Estelle and I headed in to the City as per our instructions from Draco. We left Florez the fox to guard the chicken coop. Estelle had picked up a hitchhiker, a child like 18 year old, and made her her prisoner. Estelle got special treatment because she was god at her job and it was hard to find a woman as ruthless and callous as her. A couple more girls were delivered by Draco's other crews. Florez would bathe and feed the girls in the lockup, and, I imagined, explore their more intimate attributes at the same time. Well, that was no business of mine. Only, he was playing with fire. If Draco believed Florez had disobeyed the standing orders not to molest the recruits, he would take him out in a second. But, again, that was Florez' problem. Me, I just had resort to good old Sally to relieve the pressures built up by a day of such close proximity to our imprisoned pulchritude. Sally was always there in time of need, and after the times I had spent with virtually instantaneous gratification of every sexual whim, this was a time of need.

Estelle was no help. Although she was quite a looker, she batted lefty. She was in this for the flesh. I understood from Draco that she had her own little seraglio at one of Klitzman's South American resorts. No, she wouldn't be interested in doing a guy a little favor. She'd just as soon cut 'em off and put 'em in a blender. Yeah she was a toughie. Her build wasn't exactly heavy, but, with a few more pounds and maybe an inch or two, she could play tight end for the Dallas Cowboys. She was strong and an expert in judo and karate. Thus, could she be left to handle the "guest room" alone since, even if a girl or two broke free from their chains, they would have to battle the mammaried mauler in order to escape.

I watched her that morning as she washed, fed and otherwise attended to the physical needs of her wards. One by one, the girls were stood up, hands fastened behind their backs, and taken first to the john, then the sink and then to a chair where they were given a 8 oz. glass of mush to drink. Their hoods were removed only to wash their face; the gag only long enough to drink the mush and then to have their mouths washed out and teeth cleaned. Estelle seemed to revel in her tasks and the girls were deathly afraid of her.

We left the house about two o'clock in the afternoon. We were to meet in the City with one of Draco's recruiters. We were dressed, as ordered, like a gentrified husband and wife team. Estelle wore a calf length skirt over a pair of Topsiders, with a blue and white striped blouse, her hair pulled back in a bun. Me, I was dressed in a pair of tan bucks with chinos and a crew necked polo shirt with a little animal on the breast pocket. Perfect for an informal meeting with Draco's friend.

We pulled up to a brownstone in the Village and parked in a spot which had been reserved for us by one of Draco's operatives. That was the way he was. He seemed to have a million guys working for him and you never knew when one of them would pop up. The guy on the street gave us a nod and disappeared. It was probable he had no idea what our game was. In our "club", the cognoscenti were extremely few. Mere knowledge of the nature of our operations could be a death warrant. That would be a tough penalty for double parking.

We exited the car and walked up the steps to the brownstone. A sign on the door said "Village Au Pairs".

Pairs of what, I thought, as Estelle rang the bell and we were buzzed in.

We were greeted by a receptionist, a pretty young thing, about 21 or so years old. Businesslike, she asked our names and confirmed our appointment. Within a minute we were ushered into a plush inner office, a matronly woman, about 45, rose from her desk and greeted us.

"Mr. and Mrs. Harris, so good to see you. It's been a while". A while? I had never seen this broad before in my life. Oh yeah, I got it, she was in on it. The recruiter. What a front! But how could she provide girls who could disappear without a trace? An answer came shortly.

The receptionist left the room and Estelle and the other broad made like old times. Vivian Burgess was her name, or at least the name she called herself. This was her agency and a good business it was too. But she had a little sideline it seemed and it involved us and Draco and Klitzman and the rest. She handed Estelle an 8 x 10 of a young girl, blond hair, bright, friendly eyes, an unpracticed smile. Her gaze was directly into the camera.

Estelle perused the picture like the proper judge of flesh that she was. The girl was dressed demurely enough for the purposes expressed to her I'm sure: the viewing by a prospective employer. But the dress was just slightly tight around the waist, the bodice just slightly lowered, enough so that a good measure was given of her charms. Her clean, unblemished face, fresh, bright, cheery, pure, spoke for itself. An attractive girl, eighteen, maybe nineteen. And now, in more trouble than she could have ever imagined.

There was a soft knock on the door. Vivian called for the supplicant to enter. And enter she did. The very definition of a sweet young thing. She glided gracefully across the room, her eyes directly on Vivian. She stepped up to the desk between Estelle and I. As she stood about two feet away from me I could smell the freshness of her body, a light touch of perfume. Just enough. She was wearing a red and black plaid shirtwaist dress, buttons up the front, the hem just below her knees. Her blond hair lay on her shoulders, soft, fine. Her breasts were full. Her figure was somewhat heavy, but her legs were delicate and smooth. She was trembling slightly, a movement which caused her breasts to stir gently. A small wisp of hair lay across her face. She brushed it aside. "You rang for me Mrs. Burgess?"

Ah yes, a voice as sweet and fresh as her face. Perfect. And her doom was thus sealed.

"Mr. and Mrs. Harris have need of an au pair for the summer, Cassie. They've looked over your resume and like you very much." Vivian was laying the bait.

"Yes, Mrs. Burgess, that's nice." She turned first to Estelle and then to me "I'm happy to make your acquaintance. May I ask how old your child is?" Apparently, Vivian had schooled her in the proper etiquette.

Estelle started laying it on. "Well my dear, there are two children, a little boy, Jamie, who is three, and our daughter, Lisa, who will be eight in July. We're all going to vacation in the islands for a few weeks and then we will spend the rest of the winter in Boca Raton. Do you like sailing Cassie? Can I call you that?" Cassie nodded affirmatively.

"We want to make sure that you will be responsible and take care of our children properly. Mrs. Burgess recommends you highly. Do you think that you can handle two children?"

"Oh, yes, Mrs. Harris. I have three brothers and sisters at home. I took care of them all the time."

I had been wondering what had caused this young thing to fall into Vivian's clutches and now I began to see.

Cassie had left her Midwestern home to get away from taking care of her brothers and sisters. She had probably hit town a few days ago and been handed a leaflet as she got off of the bus. "Village Au Pairs", an invitation to get herself started. A few hours of wandering around the Big Apple would surely have caused her to consider a safe harbor. And what could be safer than to be an au pair. People with children wouldn't hurt you, would they? And she knew how to take care of children. Only this time she would be paid.

"Well," Estelle continued, "we would expect you to care for the children six days a week. We'll pay double the standard rate. Your evenings after the children go to bed will be your own. But we won't tolerate any running around with boys. You can see them of course on your own time, but, well, I think you know what I mean."

"Yes, Mrs. Harris. You can be sure I'll follow your rules to the letter."

Boy, if she only knew the truth of that statement, I thought. My guess was that in about two hours she would find out.

Estelle spoke to Vivian. "She's fine, very fine. I don't think we'll need to see any of the other girls. I like her. What do you think Harry?"

I tried to act the nonplused, bored father. "Yes, yes, Estelle, if you wish. But don't forget we have to catch a plane in five hours. And we have to go home first and get the bags and the kids. Let's get on with this."

Vivian's eyes perked up. "Oh, you have to leave right away? Cassie, are your things packed? Can you leave immediately?"

"I, I ..." Cassie stuttered.

"Oh, I'm sure she can," Estelle interjected. "We'll buy her some clothes when we get there. Cassie, just throw some things together, Mrs. Burgess will take care of the rest of your things. Okay?"

Cassie tottered on the brink. The Caribbean sounded fine. Nights off, sailing, the hook went in. "Oh yes, Mrs. Harris. Just let me run upstairs and get a few things and I'll be right down."

"Fine, Cassie, fine," Vivian knew she could count her commission right now. I wonder if she was in the habit of taking Caribbean trips. If so, she might be seeing Cassie again very soon. That is, if some fat lecher hadn't bought her and taken her off into the unknown.

"I'll have the papers ready when you come downstairs. Hurry now." Vivian waived Cassie off.

Cassie spun on her heels and skipped out the door. She was obviously pleased that she had found such a great job and also probably counting her money. And to think that she had been worried about making it in New York. This was easy. A wonderful vacation ahead and a big bankroll at the end. Money would indeed change hands, and she would, I was sure, have a busy time of it.

As the girl left, Vivian and Estelle exchanged knowing glances. Vivian's real face came out. A dragon lady. She looked like she had just swallowed cream.

"I think you'll be very happy with Cassie. She needs to be thinned out a bit, but I'm sure our friends will be able to handle that." Vivian's smile could freeze butter.

"To be sure," Estelle answered her. "And I believe that you will be able to see her in a few weeks. I'm taking a few weeks off myself and I'll make arrangements for her to be available. I think her skin is quite lovely, don't you?"

Vivian nodded her assent, "It will probably bruise easily." Vivian was so practical.

I rose from my chair as I heard Cassie's footsteps come running down the stairs. The two women joined me as I headed for the door. Once outside, in the hallway, I could see Cassie holding a small suitcase, battered, with the remnants of a Winnie the Pooh sticker on the side. A childhood keepsake. I wondered if her Teddy bear was in there. Estelle would have fun with that.

The girl's chest rose and fell as she caught her breath. Would she remember with bitterness her anxiousness to be placed into bondage? As she was branded, whipped and abused, as her mouth, sex and rear were ravaged, soiled, would she think back to this moment? No doubt she would, a thousand times. But her fate was really sealed the moment she walked into Vivian's web, when she looked down at that leaflet off the bus or train as she arrived in the city, or maybe even back there in Oshkosh or wherever she was from, when she first thought wistfully of freedom, of excitement, of running away from home. Her eyes were wide with anticipation. I looked away.

"Come on Cassie, let's go. Sign the papers and let's get on our way." Estelle's first order to the slave.

Vivian placed a contract on the hallway table and Cassie placed her mark on it. Estelle and I signed too. Of course the whole thing was destined for the shredder in a few minutes. There would be no trace of Cassie left here. No evidence she had ever crossed the threshold. Vivian had a real au pair business, of course, but the real business was conducted elsewhere. Here, only the "special cases" were handled. Those who would be missed only by those hundreds or thousands of miles away, in Minnesota, Iowa, Kentucky, even California and Canada. I found out later from Estelle that she made this little trip at least once every other month, sometimes picking up pairs. Young girls harvested for the market.

As we moved toward the door and passed the young receptionist, I wondered how this voice was kept silenced about the traffic in flesh. Could Vivian keep one so close to her in the dark about her real purpose? My answer came shortly. As we passed by the slight redhead who had buzzed us through to Vivian earlier, Vivian dropped the contract which she had kept in her hand. The redhead rose swiftly and squatted to retrieve it. Her blouse rose up her back and there was a gap between it and her low slung skirt. It all became clear. There, just below her right hip, the cursive k, branded deeply. Vivian's eyes caught mine as the girl rose and handed the papers to her. She smiled. Well, Vivian wouldn't be lonely tonight.

We sped out of the city. Cassie was sitting in the back, unbeknownst to her, the doors locked, already a prisoner. I was driving and Estelle was chatting Cassie up, asking her about her past, where she had grown up, about her boyfriends, getting into her head. Cassie would soon have no secrets. Part of the training of new slaves was the complete revelation of their sexual past. One never knew what little tidbit of information could be helpful in reducing a woman to abjection. Did her boyfriend come in her mouth? Oh no? Well, to be sure, that deficiency would be remedied. Did she like it in her ass? She would be accommodated. Had she ever eaten pussy? That tendency would be happily noted. The knowledge that her most private past was as open as her body would add to the despair and hopelessness which was the precursors of submission.

Estelle tired of her cross examination of the child. We rode in silence for the rest of the way. It was dark as we reached the house. I could see the lights on upstairs as we pulled up the long driveway. Inside, the door to the secret cellar would be sealed until the identity of the newcomers was affirmed. I blinked the lights twice and the garage door slowly crept open. I drove in and turned off the engine as the door slowly fell behind me. Well, pretend time was now coming to an end.

Estelle jumped out of the car and opened the rear door. She motioned Cassie out as I opened the door to the house. Cassie followed Estelle up the short stairs to the kitchen carrying her suitcase and walked along into the living room. The shades were all drawn. Draco was sitting in an easy chair smoking. Florez was undoubtedly downstairs.

Cassie looked around quizzically at the surroundings. She was an experienced young girl. She knew that where there were children, there were toys, little chairs, little books, bicycles in the garage. And if we were so rich, why were we living in this dump? She became visibly nervous. She eyed Draco like he was a dirty cat. Estelle came in and took Cassie's bag and threw it on the sofa.

Estelle was not about to waste her time with this little piece. She was tired, I was sure, and she had a little piece of fluff waiting downstairs for her, the hitchhiker from the day before. All the day's excitement would mean a busy night for her.

Without a word, Estelle strode directly across to the girl, pulled her around to face her and then slapped her across her cheeks, the crack of flesh against flesh shattering the silence in the room. Cassie was lifted off of her feet and rolled over onto the floor. Her eyes sprang open like saucers, a large red mark already forming on her cheek. She began to cry out to protest when Estelle grabbed her hand and twisted it behind her in an expert hold. Cassie was lifted to her knees, her voice choking with the pain. Could she have possibly been prepared for this?

"Now my little pretty, we will cut out the bullshit and get down to cases." Estelle's eyes were burning brightly. She had probably been thinking about this for the last two hours. Cassie looked up at Estelle with shock and fear. Her eyes darted around the room. She looked at me and then Draco. Could she really believe that we would let Estelle do this to her? Estelle twisted Cassie's arm a little tighter causing her to squeal with pain.

"Oh, oh, please, you're hurting me. Please, let me go" Her voce was plaintive, desperate. Estelle grinned and twisted harder.

"Listen to me, little one, shut your mouth and do what I say!" The arm twisted even more.

Cassie winced with pain, her body contorted to compensate for the twisting of her arm. "I will, I will, please let me go, please!"

Estelle now pushed Cassie so that her arm was almost to the back of her neck, Cassie's face pushed down against the rug. Her squeal became a loud, painful, helpless moan.

"I said shut your mouth."

Cassie nodded yes, tears streaming down her face. It was clear to her that something awful was about to happen.

"Good. We'll get along sweetie if you keep your mouth shut and you do what you're told. Understand?"

Cassie nodded again, her eyes clenched shut, her face white.

"Now get up," Estelle ordered.

Cassie rose slowly, cautiously as Estelle lowered her arm, stopping when Cassie was halfway to her feet, bent over, looking down at the rug.

"Now, you will do exactly as I say. You will not hesitate. You will not speak. Understand?"

Cassie nodded, a slight whimper escaping her mouth.

"Good, now you will stand up, put your hands behind your head. You will keep your eyes closed and your mouth open. And you will be silent. Now do it."

Estelle released Cassie's arm and the girl gingerly rose to her full height. I could see the wetness of her face. Her body was convulsing with sobs. Her blond hair askew, no longer the neat and prim young lady. With her eyes jammed shut she slowly raised her hands over shoulders and behind her head.

"Now spread your legs apart."

Cassie complied, pulling the skirt of the dress tight.

Draco had gone back to his reading. His interest in women was individual. One on one. I had heard the agonized wails from behind his door at night back in Paliba. I had never seen him use a woman in public.

I was interested. I watched Estelle as she stepped away from her prisoner. For a moment she paused, contemplating the vignette. For only a moment. She reached into her pocketbook and pulled out a little ball gag and strap. She approached Cassie, whose trembling mouth gaped open as she had been commanded. Without ceremony, Estelle popped the gag into the girl's mouth. Pushing aside the girl's hands, she clipped the leather strap tightly about her head. Cassie's eyes blinked open in surprise. Estelle noticed and, placing her thumbs beneath the girl's jawbone, near the ear, pressed hard. Cassie sagged in pain and moaned through the gag. Her voice was deadened but her desperation was clear.

"Eyes closed honey, get it?" Estelle held the girl poised, lifting her to her tip toes. Cassie sniffled and moaned in what I could only interpret as a definite yes.

Releasing the girl, Estelle withdrew. The lights in the living room were dim, but I could see the sweat glistening on Cassie's throat and forehead. Her eyes were clamped shut as she tried to get her heaving sobs under control. It was clear that she wanted to cry out, to plead with her eyes, but, restrained by Estelle's brutality, she held herself together. She was already learning her lessons.

"Harry, make me a drink, wouldja?" Estelle had

reverted to her Bayonne twang. She plopped herself down in a chair next to Draco. When I returned a few moments later, Estelle was still staring at her young charge. The silence was undoubtedly driving the girl crazy as she wondered what was going to happen next. I was sure she could surmise that it wasn't good.

Suddenly, Estelle called out to the girl again. "Okay, sweetie, now I want you to take off all of your clothes."

The girl jumped when Estelle spoke and resumed her quiet whimpering when the nature of the order became clear to her. She had probably considered the idea that this all involved the abuse of her body. But she was also probably quite confused at how this involved Estelle. But she really didn't have time to speculate as the recollection of the painful experiences since she had entered this house were very fresh.

Her eyes still jammed shut, her mouth distended in a grotesque 'O' by her gag, Cassie drew her hands down from behind her head and slowly began to unbutton the front of her dress. Her hands trembled as she undid button after button. Tears were flowing down her face and her legs were shaking. Her plain white brassiere was slowly revealed as the dress shirt was opened. When the buttons were all released, Cassie pulled the top over her shoulders and pushed it down to her waist. She hesitated only a moment and then pushed the dress to the floor. I walked over to remove it from her feet. She flinched at my approach.

"Don't worry honey, he's not going to hurt you. Not tonight anyway." Estelle laughed. She swirled her martini and downed it at one gulp. "Now the rest, dearie. We want to see what you've got in there."

The girl quickly pulled the cups of her bra apart and pulled it off of her shoulders. Her breasts jumped free, white globes, shuddering as they moved, large pink nipples, pointed and hard. I stood only a foot away from her and I could hear her breathing, deep, frantic. I took the bra from her hands. She then hooked her thumbs in the sides of her cotton panties and pulled them down to her knees. As she was pulling them from her ankles, she stumbled. I caught her, my arms reaching around her, my hand closing over her breast. Soft, firm ample, I stroked the nipple with my finger. The girl shrank as if trying to disappear inside herself. A man's touch. A man's unwanted touch. Her first, not her last.

I took the panties from her as she regained her feet. Anticipating the order, she placed her hands behind her head again. As surmised from our interview at Vivian's, she was somewhat flabby around the middle. Baby fat. She would soon lose it as she was trained and groomed. Her pussy was covered by a thin sheen of delicate blond hair. I yearned to touch it, to part the lips and stroke the tender insides. Patience, I thought, it would come soon enough.

"Well, honey, you're going to do quite well. Good tits, nice legs. You'll lose that paunch there and you'll be quite a number. Turn around and let me see your ass," Estelle commanded. Estelle had risen to her feet and approached the sniveling girl.

Cassie turned slowly around. Her back was glistening with sweat. Her rear was pale and somewhat fatty. But an ample ass was a valuable asset to a slave, better to absorb the blows of the riding crop.

"Well, I'd say your going to get a lot of attention there too, honey. I'm, sure you'll get used to butt fucking real quick. You might even like it." Estelle ran her hand down Cassie's ass squeezing and pinching the bottom where it curved inwards, back towards the sweet little pussy in front. The girl jumped, but held her position. I assumed, but could not confirm that her eyes were still closed.

As the girl listened to Estelle, the future was now becoming clearer. Not what she had signed on for at all.

The door to the basement swung open and Florez stepped into the room. His black eyes darted over the spectacle in the living room. Even Draco had raised his head.

"A newbie eh?" Florez quipped. I could tell that his hands were itching to feel the length of her torso, the inner parts of her thighs. Mine were too.

"Take her downstairs Florez," Draco ordered. "Put her in bed three. Make sure you quiet her down too. And listen. Hands off. Got it?"

"Sure Draco, sure. I mean that's the rule, eh?" Florez chuckled.

Florez stepped forward to the girl whose back was to him. He quickly pulled her hands from behind her head and joined them at her back. He pulled a length of cord from his pocket and pulled it tight around her wrists, joining them. Her eyes popped open and then shut again and I heard a gurgle of fear from behind her gagged lips. Confinement was a lesson in subservience. Cassie was getting her first.

Florez pulled the girl around by her shoulders. He looked approvingly at her belly and breasts. He grabbed a fistful of Cassie's hair and pulled her towards the stairs. She stumbled, still clenching her eyes tightly as Estelle had ordered. She was smart. And that would help. She would not be able to avoid pain, but she could lessen it. If she stayed smart.

Florez pulled the naked girl by her hair through the door and began to lead her down the stairs, down to her future. I followed Florez downstairs to make sure that the girl made it safely to her bunk. Florez had her bent over double as he pulled her down the flight of stairs down to the landing and then over to the hidden door to the cell within. He popped the panel open and unlocked the door. He pulled her over the threshold and into the dungeon.

I would never get used to the idea of half a dozen or so naked, hooded and bound, beautiful, young women lined up in beds along the walls like patients in a public hospital ward. Most of the women were quiet. One or two were straining at their bonds, their hands chained to the wall behind them, their legs spread wide apart. The soft leather of the bracelets and anklets while protecting the skin, also made slipping out of the bonds more difficult. The leather was pulled tight to the skin, tighter than metal could be and, when mixed with the girl's sweat, tightened even further. These women were here to stay. Even if you could slip one off, there were still three more to remove before you were free of the cot. Then the hood which was locked on around the neck. Then the locked door. And then Estelle or Florez or Draco, waiting at the top of the stairs. No. These women were not going anywhere without permission.

Cassie's eyes had finally opened and she stared in disbelief. Well, I wouldn't have believed it either. She probably had never seen so many naked bodies at one time other than perhaps in the locker after gym. But those were girls. These were women, fully developed, thinned and shapely. The only one close to Cassie's age was the hitchhiker. The others ranged from about 22 to 25. If Cassie had had any doubts about her fate, they were now dispelled.

Florez pulled the girl over to the corner and commanded her to sit. As he did, I walked over to Estelle's hitcher and unlocked her bonds. I would take her upstairs to Estelle. The girl's body bore welts and bruises from her session with Estelle the night before. I did not remove the hood, but just reattached her wrists behind her back and led her by the arm to the door and the stairs above. Estelle met me at the top and crooned happily when she saw her little friend as she called her.

"Oh my goodness, what have you brought me Harry." The girl stiffened in my arms. "I think that I will retire with my little friend here for some fun and games." Estelle grabbed the girl by her nipples and squeezed. The girl moaned and flinched from the pain. Her knees gave out and I supported her with my arms. No doubt the memory of her "fun" with Estelle the night before was very unpleasant.

"Harry, be a doll and help Florez put the babes to bed," she asked, eyeing her toy. "I'll let you have a piece of my darling here a little later, after I've warmed her up a bit, okay?"

I was grateful indeed. The warmth of the girl's naked body against mine had really charged my engines.

I walked back down to the basement and entered the cell. I could hear whimpering from the other end. The cell formed an "L" and so the other end was not in my view. As I turned the corner, I could see Florez holding Cassie by the hair, bent at the waist, her head touching her knees. Her legs were spread and Florez was stroking her cunt, his fingers spreading and caressing the folds of skin on either side, the middle one manipulating the bud at the top. His thumb was in her ass.

Cassie's was whimpering and crying beneath her gag, the sound masking my entrance. I felt revolted at Florez. I had let my role playing get away with me. All sense of decency and compassion had left me. For the public good they had said. Do what must be done to learn the secrets of Klitzman's empire. Do what you have to do. I would and had. But for a moment I felt human again: shocked at the rape of an innocent girl. I grabbed Florez by the neck with my right hand and pulled him to his feet. With my left I let him have it.

Cassie fell to the floor as Florez smashed against the wall. Stunned for a moment, he recovered quickly, fire coming from his eyes. His knife was out in a second. Stupidly, in my anger I had forgotten it. All of a sudden I regretted my loss of control. Yes, this girl was suffering. But no more nor no less than she would be if I had not been here. Draco, Estelle, Vivian Burgess, they would have processed and enslaved this girl with or without me. I was jeopardizing the destruction of the greatest criminal conspiracy in history because of my sentimental compassion for this girl. Even if I had killed Florez, this girl was now either a slave or she was dead. Draco and Estelle would see to that. And now I might be dead myself.

Florez grinned stupidly at me as he swung his knife back and forth before him. I backed up slowly, looking from the corners of my eyes for a weapon. Suddenly, Florez lunged. As he did, his foot caught on the edge of one of the cots and he tumbled to the floor in front of me. I stomped my foot on his wrist, forcing the knife from his hand. He howled in pain.

I kicked the knife away from him with my other foot. His other hand grabbed for my leg. I dipped my knee on his back. He howled again. Suddenly I felt a cold steel object right behind my ear. I hear the distinct sound of a hammer being cocked. I froze.

"What the fuck is this?" It was Draco.

"Just a little fun between the boys," I replied rather jauntily considering my position. Florez had stopped howling and was struggling to get out from under my knee. Slowly I let him up.

"This bastard is going to die very soon!" Florez hissed at

me.

"I'm the one who decides who lives and dies here Florez." Draco slowly removed the gun barrel from my ear. He then noticed the girl sprawled on the floor. He said nothing. But he knew what had happened.

"Harry, get this broad to bed. Florez, get upstairs and get to bed yourself. We're driving to the checkpoint tomorrow to get set up the transfer. I want you up early and sharp. And if I find you guys fighting again, I'll kill you both. Got it?" I nodded and Florez smiled weakly.

After they left I directed my attention to the girl on the floor. She had crawled to the corner and was sobbing uncontrollably. I walked over to her and grabbed at her arm, to lift her to her feet. She fought me wildly, striking her head against the wall several times.

Taking a page from Estelle's book, a slapped her across the face, twice. This had the desired effect as she stopped struggling and collapsed in my arms. I pulled her over to the table and chair and sat her down. She needed to be sedated as quickly as possible and so I belted her into the chair and then removed her gag. She sputtered as the gag was removed. Before she could speak, I grabbed the bottle of mush from the table and plunged the end into her mouth. Its end was long and fluted so that her tongue could not bar the flow of liquid. It came with a mouthpiece which effectively prevented her from pushing the liquid out of her mouth. Because her hands were bound, I was free to hold the bottle with one hand and, with the other to hold her throat, pushing her head back.

"Drink, Cassie, drink. It won't harm you," I told her. "It will help you sleep. Put all this away for a while. You must drink." She looked into my eyes. I don't know what she saw there, perhaps a remnant of the compassion I had felt for her a few moments ago. But whatever it was she began to calm down. She drank.

I let her have a good dose. She would nod off in a few minutes so I hurried to complete my tasks. I pulled her to the shower and rinsed her down. I freed her hands from behind her back and let her rub her wrists. She looked at me with her soft, misty eyes. I cold see the thought of a plea forming in her head. I gave her a stern look which dissolved her intent.

I washed her body with all the tenderness I could muster. I soaped her breasts and belly, washed between her legs, her neck and face. I rinsed her hair and dried it. All the while, I left her hands free. Against policy, but the girl calmly accepted my instructions and ministrations. When done, I ushered her to the toilet and sat her down. She looked away as she released the liquid from her body. I handed her the toilet paper and allowed her to wipe herself. Finally, I led her back to the table and chair. Pulling a box from the cabinet, I measured her wrists and ankles. She stared glumly as I affixed the bracelets and anklets to her limbs. I prepared to apply the gag and hood. As I placed them on the table before her, she suddenly came out of her reverie and began to cry again. She could see the women in the cots. She knew what these were for and what would happen next. Darkness, silence, confinement. Her body displayed, available. For how long? How could she know? Who would she see when they were removed? Me? Florez? Estelle? I touched her cheek softly and caressed her face. I could find no words of comfort.

She spoke quietly. "Oh, mister, what is happening to me? Please help me, please?" I placed my finger across my lips, signaling her to be silent. She nodded tearfully. I took the gag from the table, gently pushed it into her open mouth and fixed it in place. Her eyes closed as I lifted the hood over her head. I covered her, buckling and locking the straps below her chin. I stood her up and walked her to an empty cot. She was trembling slightly, but lay down willingly. I guessed that the drug was taking effect, as her movements were dreamlike, slow. I snapped her wrists in place on the wall ring and then, spreading her legs, fastened her ankles to the rings on each side.

I caressed her body softly, her pale breasts, her tender thighs. I could hear soft sobs from behind the hood. I then stood and surveyed my handiwork. She looked anonymous, strange with her head bagged, her body displayed. Just like the others: breasts, a cunt, the important stuff. The difference in the color of her pubic hair, her size and shape in the end meant little. Valuable property.

The girl's rhythmic breathing told me she had fallen into a sleep. Undoubtedly her dreams would be difficult, tense. Her neighbors lay around her, their limbs pinioned, their identities masked. Bodies, not people. Recently free, soon to be enslaved. This had to end, I thought to myself, it could not go on. But to end it, it must go on. I could free them all, here tonight, perhaps, catch Draco, Estelle and Florez off guard. Maybe wait till tomorrow while Draco and Florez were out checking the rendezvous point. But, if I waited, acted only when the time was right, waited for instructions from my control before striking, maybe I could free them all, all over the globe. I could prevent hundreds, maybe thousands from suffering this same fate, save their families and loved ones from pain and dismay at their disappearance. As hard as it might be, I had to go on, unleashing the beast in myself to trap the beast that was Klitzman and his empire.

I looked down again at the prostrate girl. My heart hardened. I turned, shut off the light and locked the door.

## CHAPTER FOUR
## MARA GETS IN A LITTLE DEEPER

Only once did I come close to penetrating Nikos' well-guarded life. As usual, I had come home around 6:30. He was not there. Although many nights he would be sitting in the easy chair across from the door, smoking, drinking a tumbler of cognac, more frequently lately, he was not and arrived later, sometimes even not until after midnight. My life had become his to control, to play with. His instructions to me were that when I arrived home, regardless of where he was, I was to strip, bathe and then wait for him, kneeling at the foot of his favorite chair.

On this night, I bathed, perfumed myself as Nikos liked, and knelt waiting for him as instructed. About an hour later he entered. I could tell something was wrong. Rather than smile in contemplation of his pleasures, as he stepped through the door he was wincing, his shoulders, hunched. He nodded at me and then took his jacket off which had been draped across his shoulders and threw it to the floor. I could see the blood dripping from his shoulder. I gasped. He nodded and then walked through the living room to the bathroom. I followed him, anxiously, wanting to help, afraid to ask what had happened.

He sat on the edge of the tub and peeled his shirt off. I could see a 6" long slice at the crux of his chest and shoulder. The blood had washed down his arm and chest and had stained the top of his trousers. I rushed to the medicine cabinet and pulled out some gauze and peroxide. I washed it while he smiled ironically. My anxiety amused him.

When I got the blood washed from the wound, I could see that the cut was long but not deep. Clearly it had been made by someone slashing at him. "Nicky," I said, "you should get this stitched. This is dangerous."

"Tomorrow perhaps," he said. "Tonight I will rest here. Give me a towel, I'll stop the bleeding. You get me something to eat. I'm starved. And you must be too. Make something."

I nodded. I was speechless. What I knew of Nicky I could put in a teaspoon. I had an understanding that my life and his were different, that he belonged to a side of life I knew nothing about. But it had never been driven home so clearly, so concretely.

I rushed to the kitchen to put up some water for pasta and heated up some sauce Nicky had made the night before. I was, of course, still naked, and I felt a little silly running around nude with Nicky bleeding in the bathroom. I grabbed a robe from the bedroom and went into the living room to make sure the door was locked. I saw Nicky's jacket on the floor. I picked it up to put it on a chair. I could feel a wallet on the inside, and a small hard object in the right pocket. Nicky had told me not to ask him any questions about his life away from me, but now, my curiosity was piqued. I could hear Nicky running water in the bathroom, filing the tub. For a moment, I hesitated. Would I be betraying his trust? Would I be breaking the spell which held me to Nicky, bound me to him and his desires? But the need to know was too strong.

The right outside pocket of the jacket held a small pistol, sliver, deadly looking. My heart pounded as I felt its weight, its power in my hand. I quickly put it back. Inside I pulled the wallet from the pocket and opened it. The first thing I saw was Nicky's passport. Greek, of course. His picture inside was as dark and foreboding as I knew him to be. His name was Nikos Krikorios. I realized that I had never learned his last name before. The passport was well used, 'stamps of many countries' as the song goes. But then I found more, a Spanish identity card in the name of Nickolas Negron, a Brazilian passport in the same name. And a Byelorussian passport in the name of Nick Strakoff. All the pictures were definitely Nicky.

I was about to open the other side when I heard a movement behind me. The next thing I felt was an arm flashing around my neck, another grabbing my arm and pulling it up behind my back. I felt immediate, excruciating pain. I dropped the wallet, moaning loudly. My throat was crushed and constricted by Nicky's arm so that only a little squeak escaped. The pain in my arm was so intense I was blinded by a flash of light. In a second I was on the floor. Nicky was breathing in my ear.

"What are you doing, cunt? A little spying, perhaps?"

I struggled to deny it, to beg forgiveness to plead for air and release from pain. My need for oxygen became desperate.

"Should I just let you die here and now? I have already killed today. One more would mean nothing. Do you want to live?"

My body was convulsing now, I could sense but not see the redness of my face, the bulging of my eyes. I blubbered out my prayer for life. Nicky looked me in the eyes. I could tell he was weighing me, assessing his needs and pleasures. I only had a few seconds left when he suddenly released the pressure around my neck. My arm was held tight behind me, up around my shoulder blade. I gasped for breath, ignoring the shocks of pain which drove through me as my chest heaved.

After a few moments, I was able to blurt out a plea for release. Tears were coursing down my face. Nicky was still staring deep into my eyes. I knew I was not out of danger.

Suddenly Nicky released my arm and stood up, pulling me to my feet. Grabbing my robe's lapels with his left hand he slapped my hard across the face. I began to scream. He stifled it by closing his hand around my throat. He lifted me up on my toes. I stared helplessly at him.

For a moment I could see the anger boiling behind his eyes. And then like a shadow crossing over his face, it disappeared. He smiled slightly, lowered my off of my toes, loosened his grip around my neck. I could see that his shoulder was bleeding still.

"Now, child, can we learn a little lesson from this?" he said, a trace of humor in his voice. I nodded fearfully.

"Good. Now first of all, you are not naked. Take off your robe now." He released me and I quickly let the robe fall to the floor. I could see the blood from his shoulder smeared across the back. I worried about the rug.

"Now, I am going to finish cleaning up. I don't want to be disturbed again, understand?" I nodded again, speech being impossible for me for the time being.

Nicky reached over my shoulder and grabbed a clump of hair at the back of my neck. I flinched in anticipation of a blow, but none came. Firmly holding my head down, he pulled me out of the living room, through the kitchen and into the bedroom. I stumbled after him, fearing the worst. I still could not speak, never mind yell or scream. My heart was in my throat.

When we entered the bedroom, Nicky pulled me over to the bed and threw me down. "Stay there," he ordered.

I heard him leave the room and walk down the hall. I lay with my head covered by my arms, crying softly, my face buried in a pillow. Suddenly, he returned. "Put your arms behind you."

I complied. He tied them together with a narrow leather thong. He had never tied me before. He pulled me to my feet and pushed me back down on the bed. My hands were crushed into my back where they had been tied. As I looked up at Nicky, I could see that he had a longer, wider strap. Where he had gotten it I didn't know. Had he stocked my apartment with these things in anticipation of a day like today? I had little time to speculate as he tied one end of the strap to my left ankle. A small clasp held it in place. He then passed the end over my left shoulder and turned me over. I felt it threaded through the joinder of my wrists and then passed over my right shoulder. Flipped over again, he pulled me up off of the bed and led me back into the kitchen.

"Sit," he ordered. I complied and sat on the floor where he indicated, on the rug which ran up to the linoleum of the cooking area. The rough carpet scraped my skin as he roughly pushed me over on my back. He then pushed my left ankle up towards my shoulder. At the same time he was pulling the strap tight. I moaned in pain.

"Nicky, please, you're hurting me. Please Nicky!" My voice had returned. He ignored me and pulled my right ankle up wrapping the other end of the strap around it and pulling it tight.

I now lay on my back, my arms pulled tightly up behind me, straining my shoulders. My thighs and knees were stretched to their utmost. My sex and rear were exposed as my legs spread open, forced by the strap which connected my ankles and my bound hands behind my back. He had clipped the two leads which ran over my right and left shoulders just above my breasts and behind my neck to prevent them from slipping down over my arms. I whined in pain as the tears flowed down the sides of my face. I thought he was going to kill me.

Nicky produced a small rubber ball. He leaned over and looked into my eyes again. I was about to beg for relief from the strains of my tie, to beg for my life when he pushed it forcefully into my mouth.

"Now, I can get cleaned up," he said. "Now I am sure you will not disobey me. We will talk later."

Nicky returned to the bathroom as I strained to balance the pain between my arms and my legs. The ball stifled my moans and cries. My struggles caused me to topple over to my side which at least eased the strain on my back caused by my tied hands. Nothing could relieve the strain on my arms, forced up my back by the pull of my legs. I prayed for release, knowing that my only choice was to wait. My fate was at Nicky's pleasure.

Later that evening, after I had been released, fed, massaged, and roundly fucked, Nicky spoke to me softly. "You have learned your lesson little one?"

"Oh Nicky, I'm so sorry," I said. "I won't do it again, please believe me. I didn't mean anything, I won't do it again."

I had passively, dulled by pain and fear, permitted him to control my every move after he had untied me. Now, pathetically, I was begging him for forgiveness after being slapped, choked, and held as a painful prisoner for almost two hours. I was locked into him more than ever. He had demonstrated his power over me and I loved it.

## CHAPTER FIVE
## LOVE CONQUERS ALL

Draco had driven into the City to set up the next snatch. Only in a big city area like New York could so many girls go missing in so short a time and cause so little commotion. Of course it paid to do your homework. Some girls were more easily missed than others. Like the runaway Estelle and I had picked up at the au pair service. She wouldn't be missed much since no one knew where she was. And the doll tonight, well, I understood that she was more or less a "volunteer", a playmate of a guy called Nicky. Nicky was an independent operator, quick with a knife and mean as hell. His crime MO was simple. He picked out some rich guy and told him that if he didn't pay what Nicky wanted, he'd kill him. Some day he'd pick out the wrong guy.

The girl squirmed nervously on the black, leather limousine seat. She had long, blond hair that fell below her shoulders, almost to her elbows. It was flaxen, like spun gold, and it framed her tan, smooth skinned face like a spotlight. She was truly a golden girl. I could smell her freshness from across the seat. It smelled like a country morning, sweet and robust. She was wearing little makeup beyond the bright red lipstick and a slight blush on her cheeks. Her dress was black satin, spread like a dark pool around her, dropping down to just below her knees.

The top of the dress was joined in front in a low vee, exposing the cleavage of her ample breasts. I could see the edges of the lace bra that held them in place, lifting them slightly. The sleeves of the dress came down to her wrists, slightly puffed at the tops near her shoulders, tapering down to a closely fitted band. On her left wrist was a gold bracelet, polished smooth and shiny. On the other was a watch, golden too, but also studded with diamonds around the face. A nervous shake of her head revealed two long golden earrings descending from each ear, each one sporting a glittering blue jewel on its end, matching her sparkling blue eyes. Her legs were encased in sheer slightly black tinted stockings; her feet dipped gracefully into a pair of shiny black high heels. In other words, the girl was a knockout.

Nicky sat next to her with one of those cat swallowed the canary smiles. He was dressed to the nines as well, a flashy $1,500.00 suit, a diamond patterned silk tie, gold cufflinks. He sat with his right hand on the girl's left thigh, rubbing it gently, reassuring. He was called Nicky the Knife. A deadlier and meaner man never lived. But he was all smiles now, smiling at his new property.

Across from the lovebirds sat Draco and myself. He was watching the girl closely, eyeing her for the instrument she soon would become. I looked back at the girl. She nervously licked her lips, her eyes darting about the interior of the limo, averting them from direct contact with anyone but loverboy.

We had picked them up around eight o'clock outside one of those twenty story luxury buildings on the east side. The game plan was dinner at a little Italian place in Little Italy, quiet, at a table way in the back. At first the girl didn't know what it was all about. Some friends was all that Nicky had told her. But after the pasta and the veal, after the cappuccino and espresso had been served, along with four very full snifters of cognac, the real shit came down, or at least what passed for the real shit. Loverboy held the girl's hand and gazed into her eyes. "Mara, I told you that I wanted you to come out tonight for a special reason." Mara nodded. "I have told you that I love you more than I ever thought possible.

It's true. I need you and want you more than anything in the world. You know that."

The girl's eyes softened. "Yes, Nicky, I know that. And you know that I love you too." She smiled broadly her hand in his, stroking him softly. She glanced nervously at me and Draco. I guess we didn't look like the schmaltzy type. We weren't.

"And I've told you that I wanted to posses you, all of you, that I couldn't be happy unless I knew that you were totally mine, without reservation." She nodded slightly.

"I told you that I was yours, Nicky, and I meant it. I love you." There's one born every minute.

"And I told you that I was going to ask you to prove that to me, to prove that you are mine completely and that you would surrender yourself to me."

"I am yours Nicky, believe me."

"Please, wait till I've finished." Nicky placed his fingers over the girl's lips. She kissed them softly. "I need you to surrender your whole being to me, your flesh and your spirit. And you agreed to that. You told me that you were willing to do whatever I asked, to open yourself to me, to be possessed, even owned by me. Tonight is the night that you must show me that you meant it when you said you were mine, all mine, without reservation."

The room was still and quiet as he paused. He took a small sip from his snifter, his eyed boring into the girl's. A small drop of cognac lingered on his lip, only to be drawn in by the tip of his tongue which darted out to claim it. A snake's tongue was what came to mind.

"I have told you that part of what I will demand of you is the total surrender of your will and body to me and my desire for you. You must decide, here, tonight, now, whether these were just words to you. If they were just words, then you must say so, and I will leave you alone, step out of your life like I was never there. If they were not just words, then now is the time when you must be ready to prove this to me by accepting what I desire and demand, without question, without knowledge of what it is I will ask. Do you understand me?"

The girl's mouth was slightly agape. Suddenly this blissful and carefree night of pasta and sauce had turned into a merry-go-round spinning wildly into space. I could sense the tension in her as her lips trembled and a small tear escaped from the corner of her eye. "You know I love you Nicky. I want to be yours."

"Then you must be mine and nothing else. I've told you this a thousand times. You must accept this or we cannot go on."

"But what is it you want, Nicky? How can I say yes to something I don't even know?"

"But that's the point, isn't it Mara? You must consent to my demands, my desires before you know them. There can be no conditions, no reservations. It's all or nothing. Now, you must decide. That or the maitre'd will call you a cab and send you home. What will it be? Will you be mine?"

The girl looked around quickly. I was sure that a hundred times in the privacy of their bed she had told him she was his, that she would do anything for him. But this was different. Now she was required to say it before witnesses, not as a tender lie, a pretense, a seductive hyperbole, but for real, an oath of sorts, a surrender.

A look of fear and tension crossed the girl's face. She was clearly troubled by what her lover, or who she thought was her lover, had said. Like children, we try and wish away the unpleasant, to hope tomorrow never comes, to change what cannot be changed. It was clear that Nicky was saying exactly what he meant. Could Mara really believe him? She answered Nicky's question in a low, quiet voice, almost a whisper. "Yes, Nicky, I'll be yours, whatever you want. Just don't leave me, don't do that, please. I couldn't bear it."

Nicky beamed like a lighthouse on a foggy night. The tension in the room was cut suddenly and the mood turned festive again. Nicky boy leaned over and kissed his property full on the lips, a long hard kiss, his arm around her shoulders. "I love you Mara. You've made me so happy. You are mine, really mine." He kissed her again. Mara emerged, gasping for breath, her face flushed. She looked nervously at me and Draco. I guess our role there still wasn't quite clear to her.

Draco called for the check and placed three hundred dollars bills on the table. The maitre'd waived happily at us as we walked through the restaurant and out into the street. It was a brisk night, not really cold, but below forty. Remnants of the previous day's snow were still on the street, gray and white islands on the pavement. The limo cruised up to where we stood and the four of us got in. We pulled off.

The car was warm, almost musty. For a moment there was silence as the three men locked Mara in their gaze. Nicky was sitting next to her, doing an eyegazing routine, feeling the flesh he was soon to own. Mara may not have been briefed as to what was in store for her, but Nicky boy sure was. On his left hand I saw the distinctive Klitzman ring, the cursive K, the row of chains. Now it was Draco's turn to talk. As he did, the couple parted, the girl's eyes once more acknowledging the presence of other men, other eyes.

"Mara, I have been asked by Nicky to speak to you now about his desires for you." Draco's voice was gravelly and firm, grating, a promise of rough handling to come. No sugar coating here.

"You have promised to belong to Nicky, to be his completely and without reservation. He has explained to you that he means this in a literal sense, physically as well as emotionally. Do you understand this?"

Mara looked at Nicky, surprised. Nicky nodded, "Answer, Mara."

"Yes, I understand."

"He has requested our services in molding you, training you, so to speak, to be responsive to his desires and demands, his needs. Not only responsive, but anticipatory, disposed to please him, open to his wants in every way. Do you understand this?"

Again Mara seemed lost, she looked at Nicky, her lover, the center of her world, then at Draco, then me. What was going on here? The sands were shifting beneath her feet. "No, I don't. I don't understand." She turned to loverboy, "But I'll do whatever you ask, Nicky, I promise. Please just let me love you."

Nicky laid his hand upon Mara's face, touching her gently, turning her gaze back to his. The car sped northward back to the Upper East Side, through the amalgam of traffic and lights. It rocked us gently as it moved, the whir of the traffic, the gentle throb of the motor, dull, faint reminders that the world was still outside. A world that was being quickly made irrelevant to the young girl sitting across from me in her fine black silky dress, her long, golden legs, those crystalline blue eyes. Draco continued.

"Soon we will arrive at the place where we picked you up tonight. At that time, Nicky will leave the car and you will remain with us. You are to come with us to a place where you will be shown your duties and responsibilities. Nicky will join you there in a short while. Before he leaves the car you will perform an act of surrender to him and he will place you into our custody. Do you understand?"

Mara looked once more into the eyes of her lover. She could sense that this was the magic moment. The exact point in time when her life would change unalterably. How much, she could not be aware. Few were aware of what the 'place' Draco spoke of really was. I knew, as did the slaves who served there. No creature there enslaved could doubt the extent and degree of her servitude. Mara would learn. But for now, for this moment in time, she was suspended between two worlds. Silently, the three of us waited for her answer.

"I understand," she said haltingly, a mere murmur, but a sentence of life. It was done. Again the tension was relieved. The four of us sat silently as the car continued towards Nicky's destination and Mara's fate. Mara hugged Nicky's arm as she nestled back into her seat, resigned, lost.

We pulled up to the curb in sudden halt. The time had arrived. The girl hugged Nicky's arm harder and cried out softly, "Oh, Nicky, I love you, please believe me."

"I believe you, Mara. I really do. I can't wait to be with you again. And I will soon. I promise. But first you must fulfill your promise to me, your covenant. Will you do this?"

"Yes Nicky, yes I will, but I won't be able to bear it without you. Can't I be with you? Why do I have to go away? Please."

"You see, Mara, even now you challenge my will, my desire. Either you are mine or your are not. If you are mine, then you must obey, without question and without reservation." He held her chin in his hand as she had turned to face him. Tears rolled down her cheeks. "Now for the third and last time, do you submit your will to me, your body and soul to my sole possession, to serve me, please me and to obey me in all things?"

"Yes," she replied timidly, but clearly. The deed was done.

"Then go with these men. Obey them as you would me. It is my desire that you open yourself to them and those to whom you will be delivered so that when I come to reclaim you, you will be molded and crafted into the instrument of my pleasure that I crave and desire. Before I leave, you will remove all of your clothing and reveal yourself naked to these men, my instruments."

This was the first real act of her enslavement, a test of her commitment and understanding of what was being demanded of her. We were in the middle of the City of New York. Civilization and the rule of law were only inches away from her lovely face. True, the limo's windows were tinted and three men surrounded her, intent on her obedience to this command. But, at the same time, a yell, a scream. a pounding on the glass, these could lead to her liberation, her release. The doors were not even locked. She had no reason to assume that we wouldn't just let her go. However, should she obey this command, then she was truly lost, her will surrendered, overborne, her body and spirit not her own.

The girl looked at Nicky, her hands joined in seeming prayer before her, her lips trembling. All that society had taught her about freedom, morality, sexual equality was being weighed against her love, or passion at least, for Nicky. Suddenly, the decision was made. She shook her head sharply, tossing her hair over her shoulder and moved her hands to the back of her neck. Then she began to loosen the buttons of her dress, first the top ones, then, arching her hands behind her, the lower, down to her waist. Her actions were hurried now, almost frantic, as if she didn't want a moment's reflection to change her mind.

Her eyes averted, she pulled first one sleeve and then the other off of her arms, letting the top of the dress drop before her, into her lap. Her breasts strained at the dainty black bra which held them as she reached beneath her and pulled the dress down under her buttocks and thighs. Pushing it to her ankles, she pulled first one and then the other leg free. She hesitated momentarily, her eyes darting around the car interior but still averted from the three men who were witnessing her submission. She did not know where to place the dress. Draco took it from her and quickly placed it in a small canvass bag he pulled from beneath the seat.

The girl was lovely indeed. Her sharply accentuated waist set off her heavy, firm breasts. Her thighs were as golden as the rest of her, and as firm and taut as promised by her graceful, supple figure. She was wearing a pair of lacy black panties, bikini style, together with a garter belt of the same design. After she unfastened the stockings from the belt, she rolled them down each leg, slowly, gracefully. It was clear that she was not unused to arousing desire in men. That would not have to be taught.

I looked across at her boyfriend. His intensity was palpable as he stared at the delicate flower unfolding before us. Many times, I was sure, she had stripped for him, bared her beauteous breasts and belly, spread her legs to grant him entry to the pleasures which lay within. Her gentle mouth, the pouting lips, would certainly have caressed his cock in a loving embrace. But this time was different. Different from all that came before, not from what would come. A woman was being transformed before our eyes by her own act and deed. Her personality, her individuality, was being shoved into Draco's little canvas bag along with her clothes. She had made the last real choice she would make in her life. Her only future choices would be between pain and obedience.

The car was warm, even hot now as the tension grew. Like a moment of epiphany, the air in the limo crackled with intensity, every visual detail standing out, burning bright.

The girl paused for a moment. Obviously the real show was about to begin, the past was about to end, it all depended on your point of view. Was it the voyage or the destination which was important? No matter, they could both be enjoyed. For Mara, though, this moment would burn in her brain for a lifetime. She had a choice. Was it her nature or

Nicky's loving lies which betrayed her into choosing wrongly?

She quickly removed her bra, allowing her breasts to spring free. They were delicate, golden globes. She had apparently not been able to get a complete tan as the bottom half of her breasts, including just above her areolas and nipples was as pale as the face of a baby. Her areolas were large, the nipples unusually dark and plump for such a blond beauty. These two fine objects rocked gently as the girl lifted herself slightly from the seat and pulled off her panties. There, it was done. She was naked.

Draco noiselessly put away the panties and bra in the sack and then motioned for the girl's arm. She tenuously offered him her wrist and he undid the watch which was wrapped around it. He motioned to Mara, and she, understanding immediately, removed the earrings and necklace as well as the other bracelet which had adorned her. She handed them all to Draco who, after placing them in the bag, handed the bag to lover boy Nicky.

"Kneel on the floor of the car," Draco commanded the girl. After glancing at Nicky for assurance, she slipped to her knees. There was enough room so that she could face her lover and still be seen frontally by Draco and me. Her hair fell down across her shoulders cascading down to her breasts, partially concealing them. Draco reached down and drew her hair behind her. "Place your hands together behind you," he ordered. The girl did his bidding. Draco handed Nicky a thin leather thong and a collar of leather with a metal clasp, which was opened. He motioned to Nicky who leaned forward, his hand extended, the collar offered to the girl's neck. "With this collar, you are enslaved." Draco intoned as Nicky clamped the collar shut. "Your only duty now is to serve and obey."

Mara looked at Draco, a trace of panic. Was this the moment of reflection she wanted to avoid? Was a doubt now creeping into her mind as she exposed herself for the first time as an object, a chattel? Could she turn back time to a mere few seconds ago?

Draco proceeded with the ritual. "Your hands are no longer your own. Your master now takes them from you."

With this Nicky reached his arms around Mara as if in an embrace. Mara had allowed her arms to be placed behind her, joined, held there momentarily only by her concession to Nicky's desires. This changed as Nicky circled her wrists with the leather thong, first around them, then between. He tied it off tightly as he leaned over her shoulder to take in the visual effect of his lover in bonds, from here on in, a permanent part of her life.

Mara's torso leaned backwards as the pressure of Nicky's body forced her into an arc. Her face was a simulation of ecstasy, her eyes now closed, her lips apart. Nicky, as he finished his task, pressing her breasts close to her body with his chest, his arms around her, looking into her eyes. A long gaze and then he took her lips. The girl fairly swooned in his arms as he crushed her against him. The passion of the moment was like fire. Their mouths worked against each other as if to devour. After a few moments, they parted, Nicky releasing her lips from his. Still grasping her in his arms he said, "Are you really mine, Mara, really mine? It's a dream to me. I love you more than you can know."

Mara's eyes were watering, her chest heaved slightly. "Oh, god, Nicky, I love you too. Please come soon Nicky, I'll miss you every moment."

"I will, I will," he replied as he separated from her, sitting back down in his seat. Draco handed him a gag and hood and turned again to the girl.

"Your will is not your own so your voice must be stilled except when it is to serve your master or those who he commands you to serve." Nicky leaned over to affix the gag to her mouth. It was a simple ball gag, a rubber ball attached to a leather strap. Mara gasped as he forced the gag into her mouth. He then fastened the strap behind her head.

"Since it is not of concern to you who you serve at your master's command, your eyes see only what it is wished that you see. Thus, you master closes them." Nicky pulled the black hood over the girl's head. Our last view of her was her ached eyebrows, a sort of last minute protest as the bag slid over her features down to her neck. There it was fastened by a simple drawstring which gathered the bag together.

The boyfriend sat back for an instant, taking in the prisoner before him. Could he have ever dreamed this? Leaning over he grasped the girl's breasts in his hands. She started, the shock of this touch surprising her. I could see her hands writhing behind her back. The bag over her head was pulsing with her heavy breathing. Nicky kissed one nipple, and then the next. "Soon, my love, soon." he whispered, "Goodbye for now." Nodding briefly at Draco, he quickly exited the car.

Draco rapped at the window where Florez had sat un-seen though the partition, awaiting our pleasure. The car pulled rapidly away from the curb. Our eyes fastened on our prisoner.

The girl swayed slightly as the force of the accelerating car pushed her back. Her knees were spread far enough apart so as to keep her from falling, but the inability to use her hands to balance herself made it difficult to adjust to the car's motions. Her blond hair was splayed across her shoulders, but gathered at her throat where the black hood pulled it in. I could see the hood move in and out as the girl's rapid breathing expanded and contracted it around her nose. The effect of the gag was to heighten the sense of confinement for the girl since, in her nervous excitement, she was forced to breath only through the more constricted passage of the nose.

Already she was learning that her body was no longer under her own control.

Florez picked up speed as we drove uptown and then eastward towards our garage in the Bronx. After a few minutes of watching our new guest and student, Draco leaned over and pushed the girl gently backwards so that her shoulders and back rested against the seat. With his hands he spread her legs apart wider lowering the girl's body so that she could now rest her head on the seat behind her. The dim light of the car shone on her tanned skin and the narrow band of white around her hips and on her breasts glowed slightly. Her nipples stood out stiffly like the apexes of two soft, undulating mountains, as her breasts shuddered slightly with each small jolt and bump of the limousine. She whimpered slightly behind her gag as the posture of leaning back, her legs spread to the utmost, her arms pinioned behind her must have caused not a small bit of discomfort. Another lesson begun already.

After about a half hour we pulled up to the large bay door of our little warehouse and Florez flickered the high beams twice. The large door opened at once and the car glided in. The noise of the door closing was shattering after the quiet contemplative ride we had just experienced. Draco and I lingered briefly before moving, taking in for just an added second or two the soft lines of the body splayed out before us, the heaving chest, the beckoning thighs and breasts. Florez broke the spell by opening the front door of the limo and scurrying around to the passenger doors. He opened the one on the driver's side and Draco and I sprang into action. We pulled the girl up from her supine position and lifted her out of the car. About five feet away was the Econoline Florez had provided and we more or less carried the girl by her arms the short distance to the already opened side door. We pulled her inside and laid her on her stomach on the floor. Draco pulled out a hypo and, after carefully wiping a small area on the girl's ass, drove it home. The girl stiffened as the needle plunged into skin and a small whimper escaped from behind the gag. Draco carefully bound the girl's ankles with leather anklets which were then snapped together.

We watched as the girl's breathing became more measured and relaxed, the drug taking its effect. Draco, once he was sure the girl was under, then pulled the bag partially open, up to her nose and extracted the gag from her mouth, returning the bag over her face and drawing it shut under her chin. Florez had handed me the standard body bag was had used the other night and Draco and I rolled the girl's body into it. When finished, we zipped up the bag and pushed it into the "tool" compartment on the driver's side, locking it shut. Thus would she travel, shut into the sound proof compartment, oblivious to time and distance.

Draco shut the van doors as we stepped out and waived me and Florez towards the driver's compartment. "Get going. And take it easy."

About two hours later we were pulling in to the driveway of the split level ranch. It sat on about ten acres of wooded land. Even though it was winter, the evergreens largely hid the house from view from the road. As we turned into the driveway, Florez activated the automatic garage door opener. The van pulled into the garage and came to a stop. Florez waited for the door behind him to close before getting out. I followed suit and then swung into the back and retrieved our cargo from the side compartment.

The girl was still limp and lifting the bodybag was awkward. Florez and I swiftly carried the bag from the van and into the house through a door which communicated with the house. As we crossed the threshold I saw Estelle holding the door for us, gazing curiously at our burden.

"Well, a nice day's work I see."

"Yeah," I said, "a nice day's work. One more for the collection. Open the cellar door."

Estelle opened the cellar door and led the way down the short set of stairs. At the bottom was the steel cased door with a deadbolt attached. Estelle pulled out the key and turned the lock. The three of us passed in. The room was dark as pitch black coal, lit only by the column of light which entered through the door which had been just opened. Estelle flicked on a light switch by the door as Florez and I passed into the room.

Florez and I carried our package over to the first empty mattress and placed it on the floor gently. I unzipped it and Florez and I removed the body inside. Quickly, we unchained her hands from behind her and attached them to the ring at the head of the mattress. Estelle had grabbed her legs and, after affixing the confining anklets to them, clipped them onto the rings on the floor. We all stood momentarily admiring the fine, tanned body displayed beneath us, as the young girl moaned slightly, apparently coming out of the drug induced stupor in which she had made the trip to our little hideaway.

"Yes, a nice day's work," Estelle said quietly. "Very nice indeed. Here, help me with the hood." She spoke to Florez. Florez grinned.

"My pleasure," Florez answered. "I didn't get a chance to get a good look at this baby yet. I like to see what our merchandise looks like so I can put in my reservation when we get to the island." He chuckled.

Estelle pulled off the hood which Nicky had placed on the girl in the car while Florez held her head up off of the mattress. "Oh, what a pretty one," he said. "Waking up now, my pretty one?"

The girl was stirring, her eyes slowly focusing on the leering face above her. Her body stiffened suddenly as her mind registered what her senses were taking in. Estelle had slipped the gag back into her mouth. It suppressed her gasp as Florez's hands pulled her face close to his. Her eyes, wide now, fixed on Florez's face. Florez, keeping one hand behind her head, slowly drew the other across her neck, down to her breasts, stopping briefly to gently test their firmness, and then descended to her belly and the mound between her thighs. "Oh, yes, I'll be seeing more of you," Florez whispered to the girl menacingly. "We'll do a little dance together, chicita, a long, slow one."

"Come on now, cut the play. I've got to get this one bedded down and out for the night. You know the rules." Estelle kicked gently at Florez who was now probing the girl's loins, grinning, devouring the girl with his eyes. Florez looked up at Estelle.

"Sure honey, I'll play by the rules. I can't help myself." He laughed as he withdrew his hand from the girl's pussy, and lifted her head so that Estelle could place a new hood over her face. The new hood differed from the one Draco had given Nicky in the limo in that it was heavily padded, but with a mesh over the face by the mouth and nose. Clearly, the hood was to prevent the girl from damaging herself by banging her head against the wall or floor, assuming she could reach it. The mesh ensured that her breathing would not be cut off.

Having replaced the hood, Estelle produced a small object from the pocket of her skirt and, tearing off its cover, knelt down next to the girl. She gently parted the lips of the girl's vagina and inserted the object inside. She looked up at me as she pushed her finger deep inside the struggling form on the floor. "Suppository," she said. "Keeps them very mellow."

I looked over at the other forms on the floor. Mellow was the word. The five other females were lying quietly on their mattresses, an occasional moan the only sound. Yes, mellow was the word. These creatures should be thrashing and screaming, imprisoned in a nightmare, at the most days before, free and unfettered, their lives and their bodies their own. But now, confined, stolen, their ultimate fate unknown to them, panic and fear the only emotions which would suit what their minds could fathom of what had happened, what was happening to them. Mellow, yeah, for now, but they would need to learn another state of mind soon, obedience, instant, reflexive, unquestioning obedience.

I looked around the room. Two mattresses down from the new girl I saw the girl we had boosted from her own apartment a couple of nights ago. I could see it was her from her well muscled body and the blond pubic hairs. No mistaking that body. Two days in chains. Mellow, yes, and an unwitting kindness, as these girls awaited their fates. Estelle rose from the floor and motioned us out of the room. As we passed through the door, her arm swept the light switch off and darkness and silence again invaded the below ground prison. The last sounds the chained and drugged women would hear, other than their own stifled moans and pleas, was the slam of the door, the rattle of the lock as the bolt was shot home.

## CHAPTER SIX
## MARA'S SURRENDER

After that episode I felt totally at Nicky's mercy. I did not want to live without the thrill he gave me, the electric charge of danger and the unknown. Since that night, he regularly kept me tied and gagged while he cooked, showered or even slept. One night he left me hogtied in the middle of the living room all night while he went out to god knows where. His attitude was different, colder, more aloof than he had been even before. I felt him slipping away from me. I was desperate at the thought that he would leave me. Each time he entered my apartment, I thrilled anew at his presence. Each time he was late, or even those few nights that he did not come, I spent my time agonizing, praying that I had not seen him for the last time.

And so finally the day came when he called and told me we were going downtown to a little Italian restaurant I had never been to before. He had called me at work. My vacation was just starting. He had told me to take it, no explanation offered, none demanded. He wanted me, that's all I knew. I assumed we would go away. In my mind, I imagined two weeks of intense pleasure and yes, pain. Nicky had not struck me again since that first night, but I knew that a barrier had been broken. I could see in my mind the satisfaction on his face that night when he had slapped me. I didn't care. I had truly never felt so alive before, so excited. I was living on a razor's edge and I loved it.

I had packed my bag on his instructions the night before. We would meet at my apartment after work. At work I just told them I was going away for two weeks, 'going on the road' I called it, away from phones, bosses and clients. I hadn't told anyone about Nicky, his shadowy existence stifled the usual girl talk. I knew that my focus on Nicky and our sexuality was fragile, could dissipate at a moment's notice, one word of alarm from a friend, one wide eyed look from a coworker, would be all that was needed to burst this fantastic bubble. And, most importantly, I hadn't talked about Nicky because he had told me not to.

When I got home, I showered and perfumed myself, as he liked. I dressed nervously. Nicky had asked that I dress simply, but elegantly, that we were to meet some of his friends.

I feared this and wanted it. Nicky's friends, who would they turn out to be? Why did he want me to meet them? Why, on the cusp of my vacation, were we breaking our routine, going out, meeting people. With trembling hands I put on my sapphire earrings, matching watch, and golden bracelet, all remnants of a woman I used to be. A black, short dress, simple, revealing. I brushed my long blonde hair, penciled in my eyeliner and lipstick, perfumed my neck, between my breasts and hands. I dabbed a little at the top of my thighs. Nicky had bought it. He liked to smell it on me, on my intimate parts, my breasts, my vulva, my thighs. Slipping on my nylons, I was ready. Nicky had told me to meet him downstairs. I left my bags in the apartment. I figured that we would either stop by and pick it up after dinner or sleep there and leave in the morning. Nicky hadn't told me more than to be ready.

We were picked up by a long, black limousine. It drove us to Little Italy and let us out in front of the restaurant. Nicky's friends were already inside.

The dinner was long, leisurely. The three men, Nicky and his friends, Harry and Draco he called them, spoke of business, vague affairs, savoring their meals and, I could see, me. I sat next to the one called Harry, across from Draco, on Nicky's left. More than once I felt their eyes piercing me, cutting through me, while I, frightened, lost, had eyes only for Nicky. After dinner, as he spoke to me, my stomach, although full, wrenched as if empty. Yes, I did love him. Yes I would do anything for him. Why did he have to ask? Why did I have to make these declarations before these two dark and threatening men?

Yes, I told him, I was his without reservation, Yes I would prove it if he demanded it. Here? Now? How? Why? I wasn't to be told. Later, I guessed, I would be shown. It was now or never. No don't leave me Nicky, don't abandon me, I need you, I'll die for you, do anything. All these things raced through my mind. My mouth was as dry as a hot box, sweat running down my ribs, perspiration across my brow. Harry and Draco staring at me, awaiting my declaration. Clearly, this involved these men. What this meant to Nicky I didn't know. But he couldn't leave me, he mustn't. I couldn't live without him.

Finally I was able to squeak out a reply. "Yes, Nicky, I'll be yours, whatever you want. Just don't leave me, don't do that please. I couldn't bear it."

The tension around the table was broken, Nicky was beaming at me, his arm draped across my shoulders, he kissed me. Somehow, I knew I was lost.

The next part seems all of a blur. We were in the limo, speeding uptown. Draco was talking, Nicky caressing me. I was to go with them. Where? Why? For how long? Questions I knew I should ask. But questions I knew I couldn't. I had surrendered myself to Nicky and his will.

Whatever was asked, whatever demanded, in his name, I would do.

Suddenly the limo pulled to a stop. Surrender, an act of surrender was demanded. What would that be? Disrobe, undress, needless to say, of course, I had done this for Nicky a hundred times, but these men....

I was not a virgin when I met Nicky, far from it. I had undressed before a dozen lovers over the years since I had turned old enough to vote. But never before more than a single man at a time. Never before anyone who gazed at me with such cruel and cold eyes as these friends of Nicky's. Yes, I hesitated, yes, I tried to negotiate, press for advantage, would he really make me do it, did he really mean it? Nicky's tone told me that he did. What choice did I have?

It was the shorter man, Draco, who explained it. I couldn't believe my ears. I looked at Nicky. If I said no, this would be the last time I saw him. My entire being revolted at such a possibility. I looked at the two strange men. I was going to go with them. They would turn me into Nicky's whore. I wanted to be his whore, more than anything else in the world. If surrendering to these men meant that I would achieve that, I would do it.

After I expressed my timid consent, I was told to take off my clothes.

When I was naked, my clothes taken from me, my jewelry stripped from me, I knelt on the floor of the car, Nicky on my left, the two strangers on my right. Something was handed to Nicky, my hands pulled behind me, my breasts thrust out. Nicky leaned over. As he put it on me, the mean looking one, Draco, said "With this collar you are enslaved."

Enslaved? A bolt of panic struck through me. I looked around at the hard faces of the three men. What was happening to me? He had placed a thick leather collar around my neck. I couldn't see it, but its roughness scratched at my skin, my throat, tensed, constricted.

Nicky leaned over again, embracing me. I felt my hands behind me being drawn together, tied, joined as my nipples pressed against his suit, my breasts crushed, my thighs tight against his. Still, I didn't struggle. How could I? Nicky wanted this. I loved Nicky. I wanted this too. He kissed me. I drank in his kiss like a woman dying of thirst. I needed to feel this anchor while the rest of me was slipping away. The fire lit in me as always, through my insides to my loins. My hands squirmed, unused to bindings, wanting to return the caress, to bring my body even closer to Nicky's. Suddenly, he pulled back.

It was then I felt myself, drifting, dizzy, floating away from one world into another. I was to be a slave. A slave, owned by Nicky, not what I had dreamed of, not what I had wanted. But Nicky's love, yes, that was what I wanted. But at what price? That decision had been made. Trembling, not fully believing what my senses told me was happening, I told Nicky I loved him. My hands had been taken from me, given to Nicky. Draco then showed me a gag and handed it to Nicky. A ball dangling midway on a leather string. Now my voice was being stripped away. "Not gagged!" I thought, I couldn't stand that. I was going along, I was doing what was told. Not a gag! Oh, please! These thoughts were barely across my mind when Nicky pushed the ball gag into my mouth, past my teeth, filling it my mouth, pressing down my tongue, stretching the muscles of my jaw. Quickly, with practiced motion, the strap was clasped behind my neck. My heart jumped. No, no, this was wrong. I didn't mean it, what I had said, what I agreed to! I can't have this happen, please Nicky, please don't make this happen, please!

My mind screamed, my voice was lost, mere murmurings. The gag suppressed the last expression of my will, my hands frozen helplessly behind my back, my voice stilled. I pleaded with the only thing I had left, my eyes. And then all went black. A hood was pulled over my head, my last view of the world as a free woman, Nicky's face, denied me, all reassurance now gone. I panicked. Suddenly hands pressed against my breasts, Nicky's? His voice, soft, reassuring, his lips on my nipples, he loved me, I was his, he would reclaim me, he said. Oh, god, make it true.

And then he was gone. The car sped up, I was alone with my captors, naked, bound, silenced. I knew they were staring at my breasts, my belly, my thighs. How could they not. I knew I was physically desirable, hadn't Nicky and others told me countless times before. But now, these charms, as they were, were displayed to men who had no need to flatter me, to cajole, caress, persuade. I was in their power, physically and emotionally. I strained at my bonds, no, no, no, this was a mistake, wrong. Let me go, let me go.

Hands then touched me, not to free me, but to push me back against the seat, spread my legs, lean me back. My back muscles strained, I moaned. My body was as taut as a bowstring, my nerves on end. But then, the rocking of the car, the gentle hum of the engine, the softness of the seat on my back and head as I knelt back, calmed me, settled me. I was lost, my fate sealed, no need to act, no need to think. I let myself float into semiconsciousness.

I don't know how long it was before I was transferred from the limo to another car or van. Doors slamming, arms lifting me, pulling me from the car. Concrete under my feet, then up a step and onto my stomach, a shot, oblivion.

I awoke still bound and gagged, hooded and laying on my back on a lumpy mattress of some kind. My hands bound above me, fixed to the headboard or the wall or such, my feet spread apart fixed to the sides of the bed. The room, wherever it was, was quiet. I was still groggy, but, as I struggled to consciousness, I remembered what had happened, what I had become. But what was I doing here, wherever that was? What was happening to me? I could sense more than hear the presence of others in the room. A slight moan to my left, a rattle of a chain to my right. The room was warm, almost steamy. An echo, stone walls? The word dungeon came into my mind.

I lay there pulling occasionally against my bonds, straining at the gag in my mouth aching to pull my legs together. I knew I had been out for a long time, but what was going to happen to me I didn't know, or else I did and I didn't believe it. I couldn't help but crying, calling out for Nicky, my mother, my father anyone to help. This could not be happening to me, a twenty first century woman of education, ambition, articulate and empowered. My fate was my own, I had thought. I would decide and fulfill my destiny, whatever that was. But then, this was my choice, my decision. I could have walked out of that restaurant at any time. No one forced me into that car, no one forced the words of surrender from my mouth. My destiny, had I fulfilled it at last? Was I a slave to my passion, my need to feel it to evoke it? I began to cry.

Some time later, with a clang and a bang, a door opened. Voices entered the room, a man, a woman, laughter. I could hear them approach my bed. I had never felt this kind of fear before. What had Nikki meted out for me? Were these his agents, his messengers? What was going to happen?

Hands on my hands, hands on my feet, unfastening them from the bed and wall. I was pulled up to my feet unceremoniously. My legs were like rubber as I leaned

against a shoulder (whose?) and was pulled along the floor.
I tried to push my self away, to strike out, more laughter,
male and female. My hands pulled behind me, retied, a
hand between my thighs, pulling the hairs there, urging me
forward. I was defeated.

I felt a seat beneath me, a toilet. Oh what a relief as I
emptied my bladder. I was almost grateful. As I finished
my pee, I was pulled forward, my backside exposed. As I
was held tightly in a man's arms, I felt a nozzle enter my
behind, a warm gentle pressure inside me and then a flood.
I tried to pull away, but, held there, was subjected to three
more assaults, each producing a stream of waste and fetid
air. The man and woman who held me exchanged witty
remarks as they cleaned me up. A man's hand twisted my
breasts, ran itself between my thighs. Oh, god, no, not that,
I thought. But it was not to be, not yet.

After drying me off, the two pulled me to a chair and
pushed me into it. My hood suddenly lifted, the straps on
my gag loosened. A stout, middle aged white woman, a
cheesy type, sat before me. She wore a simple housedress,
her hair, pulled back, shoulder length, brown and dirty.
Her face was rough, snarly, a person to fear. Her appearance complimented the prison like surroundings. She held
a bowl and a spoon. I was to be fed. "Now dearie," it was
the woman speaking. "We can do this the easy way or the
hard way. You can keep quiet, eat your food and we'll all
stay friends. Or I can get this stuff inside you the hard way
and then have a little fun teaching you some manners. Got
me?"

I nodded. The gag was pulled out. A spoon shoved in.
Some kind of mush, bitter, rough. My stomach wanted it,
my nose said no. My stomach won.

As I finished the bowl, I took in my surroundings. A
long, narrow basement, ten beds head into the stone wall.

Five were full, hooded, naked women, bound as I had been, splayed across them. My mind reeled. Where was I, what was happening? Whatever it was, it was hard and cruel. These people were hard and cruel. Was this my destination? Would I see Nicky here soon? What would these people do to me?

After the bowl was finished, the woman passed a plastic bottle to my lips. I drank greedily. I don't know how long it had been since I had eaten or drank, how long I had been asleep, but my arms and legs ached, my throat was parched. The liquid, cool and smooth, fruity, tasted like a nectar. I gobbled it down greedily. The bottle was then pulled away. The woman smiled, the man, a dark Hispanic type, leered. What would happen now?

I was pulled to my feet and returned to my bed. The gag and hood replaced. The man held me as the woman untied my hands and, pulled my arms and torso from side to side stretching me, relieving my cramps. Then on the bed, my legs pulled up, stretched, pulled, massaged. I have to confess that it felt good. My hands then were retied to the wall, my legs stretched apart. I felt a hand, a large rough hand push aside my lower lips, caress the furrow between them. An expert's caress, I felt myself lubricate and a thick finger slide in. I gasped behind the gag. Not this, not now, please, I thought. But my thoughts were getting foggy, my mind numb, I tried to press my knees together feebly.

A voice shot out, the woman's, "Hey asshole, get your fuckin' hand outta there." A man's laugh, the hand withdrew.

As I lay there, I could hear the other women lifted one at a time from their beds and serviced as I had been. One woman begged and pleaded to be released, tried to bargain, cried. Two loud slaps and then the voice was stifled quickly. The next sounds were her muffled moans as I heard the man and woman struggling to push something down her throat. "Now you'll eat, you bitch", the man speaking. Silence and then whimpering. Eating was not discretionary.

I don't know how long I was there, how many times I was serviced by one or the other the woman, the man. I lost track of time as the mild tranquillizer in the drink they gave me caused me to fade in and out of consciousness. Every few hours, one of them slipped something into my vagina, a suppository, I supposed, and soon after I was sleepy again. I could see during my little meals that the beds were being filled with another two added, women, girls really, affixed to each.

Once, when the woman came to service us, she was accompanied by a young girl. The girl wore a collar and bracelets of leather and steel. She was naked, her eyes red from crying. From her tiny breasts and slender build I guessed that she was no more than eighteen. She was gagged, a chain connecting her ankles. Red welts stretched across her small breasts and her thighs. She helped as I was stretched, fed and emptied of wastes, working silently. I could read the pleading in her eyes as she washed me, fed me. In my torpor, I had no sympathy for her. But the image of her delicate frame, crisscrossed by the evidence of her abuse burned into my brain. When would I feel the lash? I began to tremble with fear as I was led back to my bed. Was this what Nicky wanted? Would he be the one to stripe my body with welts? Would I be able to stand it or would I die from terror and pain?

As I lay in my bed, drifting in and out of drug induced consciousness, I desperately ran through the various things I could do to escape, to get away. Then I imagined being reunited with Nicky, remembered my passion for him, cried, pitying myself and where my foolishness had led. The fear of the unknown. Fear of fear itself. I was physically so weak that overpowering the woman or the man who took care of me was out of the question. My hands and legs were firmly secured. I could not cry out. I was truly helpless, unable to prevent whatever it was that they were going to impose. What were they waiting for?

Only once was the routine of my servicing varied. A door opened, a man entered. He softly closed it behind him. I heard him walk up to my bed. He sat next to me. I waited for my hands to be unfastened, but something else was in store for me. I felt the man lean over my body. A quiet, gravelly voice, accented, whispered to me, "Oh, my lovely one, how are you today? I think you are wasting away here. Are they saving you up?" A hand drifted across my breasts, my stomach. "How is your little cunt feeling, hey?" The voice continued, "What do you say we have a little party, yes?"

His hand came to rest on my vagina, his fingers roughly prying the lips apart, pushing in, burning me. I moaned in pain. "I am going to suck your pretty little cunt dry," he said.

I tensed, pulling at my bonds, flexing my legs, trying to pull them together, to deny him access to my self, my innerness. In vain. I felt his hand float gently down my thigh, his lips press against my stomach, across the forest of hair above my private place, my treasure, my crux of love as Nicky had called it. My thighs were pulled apart by my bonds, lips fastened on me below.

In spite of myself, I felt a warmth float up from my thighs through my body to my breasts and into my brain. His tongue darted across my clitoris along the outside and inside of the lips, inside deep into me. His hand found my breasts and squeezed them, at first gently, and then harder and harder.

Unconsciously I began to thrust my hips towards him, wanting and not wanting him. In spite of myself, I felt the familiar feeling rise, my heart beating, drumming in my brain. The tongue was flitting over my clit like the wings of a butterfly. Finally, exhaling a low moan, pulling at the bindings on my hands and feet, I came. As I did, I was exhilarated and forlorn at the same time. Denied my own will, I had nonetheless been brought to the extreme of physical pleasure. No consent asked, none needed.

The man rose from my thighs, caressing my breasts and belly. "You're a hot one bitch," he said. "I'll be seeing more of you." He slipped a thumb inside me. "Soon that will be my cock. But for now, I think I will delight myself with one of these other beauties. Thanks for the warmup."

He left and I could here him speaking low to another of the inmates of this little dungeon. A short while and I could hear the sound of rhythmic thumping of flesh on flesh, a low moan, trailing on and off, a female moan, a helpless moan. A few minutes and then silence. The man quietly left. The only sound then was a girl's whimpering. It took me a few minutes to realize that the whimpering girl was me.

Finally, the day came when everything was different. My best guess was that I lay there the better part of four days, serviced three or four times every day. By that time, I could no longer put two thoughts together. My mind was befogged by the drugs I was being fed, the torpor of being confined, imprisoned. I could no longer understand the voices as they spoke out of the darkness which constantly surrounded me. I knew something was happening. People were coming in and out, bodies being moved. Soft whimpering, laughter. My turn came.

I was lifted from the bed and pulled, first to the toilet, then to eat some mush and then out the door. I leapt for joy within myself as I was dragged past the empty bed which had been my prison. The hood was off, the gag still in. My joy was short lived however as I saw as I entered the next room, a row of wooden coffins, three of them filled with the bodies of my sister prisoners. Oh, God, I thought, they're going to kill me. They're going to bury me alive! I tried to struggle. I looked around for a sympathetic face. Three men and the woman, all deadpan, all businesslike. What had I done to deserve this?

I didn't have time for further speculation since I was pulled over to an empty coffin. I was then unceremoniously dumped inside. My legs were affixed to clasps on the sides, as were my wrists near my hips. Straps were pulled around my ankles, thighs waist and neck. My gag was pulled out, and a mask pushed on my face, with a mouthpiece which filled my mouth and stilled my attempt to cry out.

I heard a voice say, "Okay, let's get these four out and then do the next."

As a lid was lowered on top of my coffin, I struggled desperately at my bonds. "Oh, my god," I thought, "please help me!" This was the worst fear of all, being buried alive. Of all the things that came later, all the pain and humiliation I suffered, all the long days and nights of servitude, this was the lowest, the most terrible moment of all. "No, no, it couldn't be!" my mind raced. "But what was happening? Where was I being taken?"

I felt myself being lifted, carried up a short set of stairs, along for a ways and then lifted. I felt the coffin being placed down. I could hear nothing outside, not a squeak. I was sure no one could hear any small noise I could make. But it still took all of my strength to restrain myself from calling out, screaming from behind my gag. Consciously, I knew that I couldn't have been kidnapped, confined, coddled and cared for just to be dumped somewhere in a grave. But how could I be sure? And what could I do about it? These questions terrified me. I felt, rather than heard something being laid on top of my box. Another coffin? And then a motor's vibrations, we were in a truck. We began to move.

An hour, two, later, I don't know, as the mush I had been fed had its soporific effect on me, the truck stopped. After a while, I felt the box above me being lifted, and then mine. Whoever was doing this seemed to be in a hurry as I was tossed around and even dropped at one point. I was lifted again, placed down, slid along a smooth, flat surface, and then, again silence. All this time I had been able to breathe from the tube placed in my mouth which led to the exterior of the box. But now something different was happening. A sour taste entered my mouth, being gently blown in. I fought it, tried to spit out the tube, rolled my head from side to side. In the end, I had no choice but to breath in the fumes. A momentary shudder went through my system, and then, nothing.

## CHAPTER SEVEN
## HARRY'S TALE: DOUGIE'S GIRL

The house was set back from the road about two miles. I sat in the front seat of Draco's black Caddy as Rodriguez and the two Mau Maus followed in the van. We had serious business here today and Draco had brought the heavies.

I had been in country, so to speak for about six weeks. After we had shipped off the captured women from New York, we moved on to Atlanta. The principal crew came with us. Draco had a back up crew almost everywhere.

While we were on the hunt, from time to time, we did some other jobs for our fat employer. This was one of them.

We cruised slowly down the dirt road serving as the driveway. There had been a soft rain about an hour or two before and the dust thrown up by the advancing cars was minimal. About a mile and a half in, Draco pulled the Caddy to the side of the road and slid it into a small copse of trees. There was just enough room for Rodriguez to pull the van in behind us.

As we got out, I patted my side in assurance. It was nice to feel the heft of my "enforcer" strapped to my shoulder. Draco didn't like gunplay but it was best to be prepared. We were there to settle a little "collection" matter and the collectee might have a small objection to our techniques. Our plan was simple: get the dough and then blow the guy away.

The collectee was a small drug operator who had amassed a small fortune in collectables. It seems one of his loads had been seized by DEA agents a few weeks before and this guy seemed to feel that this cancelled out his obligation to pay. He was already into Klitzman for a couple hundred grand and this load put the debt up to about 300K. Now we could not be sure that this kind of money would be lying about the house, but we had ways of encouraging Mr. Dopester to go get whatever was not at hand. Before we had left the garage, Draco had showed us the photo of Dopester's girlfriend, a friendly looking blonde, youthful, attractive. She would make excellent collateral. We were coming to collect her.

Draco motioned for me to follow him as he walked slowly through the woods to make an oblique approach to the house. It was a little after 5 A.M. and buddy boy and his girl, even if they had had an evening of revelry, were certainly fast asleep. We didn't know for sure that they were there, but if they weren't, well, we would be back tomorrow.

The two tall and heavyset enforcers Draco had brought with us were on his regular taxi squad. I had seen one, a few days before, squeeze the life out of a petty second story guy who had tried to pass off some questionable goods to one of Klitzman's fences downtown. It was lucky that we had the hot sheets from the Atlanta Detective's Bureau. The problem was that the stuff wasn't on the list. If it wasn't on the list it meant that it wasn't stolen. If it wasn't stolen, then our boy was setting us up. His body had been found by the lieutenant in charge of the investigation in his trunk when he went to fix a flat tire. Surprise!

The light was just beginning to show in the east and Draco signaled us to get moving. Slowly and quietly we stalked the house. There was a small rise before the walkway that led to the front door. As we reached the top of the rise, Draco signaled Mau Mau one, the smaller of the two, if smaller was the right word, to advance to the side of the house where the alarm system could be overcome. It seems that every system devised by human ingenuity can be overcome with more ingenuity. The Mau Mau, his nom de guerre was actually Remo, had a small black box which would override the signal from the alarm. At alarm central, the signal would continue to run smooth and clear.

We gave Remo about five minutes to complete his work. Draco then signaled Genda, the other Mau Mau, to ease around the other side to cover the back of the house. He would enter the house through the patio door. We would approach the front and Remo would slide in the basement. A three way assault.

Draco and I strolled nonchalantly up the walkway. With the alarms off, and the phones cut, there was no need for stealth. I had imagined that we would jimmy the front door and surprise little missy and the bad boy at rest, but Draco had other ideas. He rang the bell!

I looked at him like he was crazy, but he just shrugged. Nothing happened for a minute or so and so he rang the bell again. A few moments later I could see through the curtained window in the door that someone was approaching. Although I couldn't make out any features, it seemed that it was our target, the dopester's squeeze.

Pushing the curtain aside, she peered out of the doorway window. Draco smiled and pulled out a facsimile of a FBI badge. Nice to have that kind of thing isn't it?

Seeing the badge, the girl did what most red blooded Americans would do when a cop came to their door, she opened it. Since she had to know the dopester's means of support, she probably believed that the house was clean. In any case, since we were cops, or so she thought, we would probably bust our way in anyway. So why not open up and see what the problem was?

Sleepy eyed, the girl's face poked out from behind the door and surveyed us. She had close cropped blonde hair and her face was round and cute with a dainty little nose. She led off with the standard phraseology.

"What do you want?"

"A few questions, ma'm. Are you Amy Davidson?"

"Yes."

"May we come in?"

"No."

"Can you step outside?"

"No."

"Is Mr. Martin home?"

"No."

The girl's tone was getting petulant. Well, that would be taken care of shortly.

"Listen, you've got a lot of nerve waking me up at five o'clock in the morning to ask me some stupid questions," she said. "Now, if you don't have a warrant, I'm going back to bed."

"Well, I do have something." Draco replied as he reached into his inside coat pocket. The girl's eyes went to Draco's hand as he reached, but, the hand being quicker than the eye, a split second later Draco's switchblade knife was under her chin, its point making a little indentation, just enough to be noticed. It was noticed.

The girl stepped back quickly trying to swing the door shut. It was too late as I had grabbed the door handle and held it firmly. Draco jumped into the house, following the girl and pressing forward with his blade. The girl's head was tilted backwards as she attempted to relieve the pressure of the knife point under her chin. She was about to turn and run when she backed up against Remo. It was like hitting a brick wall.

"Now, now, Ms. Davidson, don't get all out of joint,"

Draco told her. "We're friends of Mr. Martin. Business partners. We're just here to collect a little debt he owes us. I know you can be helpful. What do you think?"

The girl's eyes were wide with terror and surprise. Remo had fastened his hands on her shoulders and then slid down her arms to imprison her wrists. He drew them behind her back.

"P,p,p,please, don't hurt me, please." Her voice trembled.

"Oh, we're not going to hurt you, Amy. I may call you Amy, mayn't I? I think that you will cooperate with us now, won't you?"

"Y,y,yes," she stuttered.

"Good. Now let's step back into the house and we can have our little talk."

The girl backed up, guided by Remo behind her and encouraged by the tip of Draco's knife. I closed the door behind me and checked for any busybodies through the window. None.

The foyer led into a short hallway. To our right were a small set of steps that led down into a large den-like room. Furnished in a colonial style, the room had a large fireplace at one end and large comfy chairs along the wall. There was a long, low wooden table, a refinished ship's hatch, gleaming with polish, brass handles fixed in the wood in each corner. A large beam crossed the room at the ceiling. A couch backed up against the large picture window which looked out into the front yard. With an ornate wooden frame, large overstuffed pillows and a delicate blue fabric, it looked comfy indeed. Remo pulled the girl into the center of the room and then stepped away from her. Draco relieved the pressure of the knife from her chin and let her take a step back.

Surrounded by invaders, our little Amy knew she wasn't

going anywhere. She looked around her furtively, getting a good eyeful of Remo's bulk and then returning her gaze to us. Her eyes glanced quickly to her left at the telephone sitting on a small end table next to the couch and then to the wall behind us. I followed her gaze and saw the panic button alarm encased in the wall just past the entranceway. Draco saw it too.

"Now so you know, Amy, the alarm has been disconnected and the phone wires are cut. So let's not have any heroics. You can try to jump through the window, but that looks like it would hurt a lot. And, since this isn't the movies, you might not make it through. You would just get all cut up and we would be pissed as hell. So let's just relax a little ok?"

The girl nodded dolefully.

I was now able to get a good look at our new friend. She was about 5'6, a little heavy boned, but shaped just right. She was wearing a dark red paisley robe, tied at her middle with a matching sash. I could see a pale green nightie underneath. The robe went to the floor, covering the tops of her feet which were bare. A nice turquoise polish was on her toenails, matching the nails on the tips of her hands. Her hair was straw colored, little ringlets at her forehead instead of bangs. No makeup, but her lips were dark red. Her eyes were green, but with a hazel tint. Her heaving chest, brought on no doubt by incipient panic, revealed an ample bosom. Well, we would see.

Draco broke the silence. "Now Amy, we need to get a little comfy here and I think that you are a mite overdressed for the occasion. So I'm going to ask you to take off your robe so we can get a better look at you." He waved the knife nonchalantly. "Of course, we can assist you if you would like, but we really don't want a scene. Do you?"

The girl was trembling, her arms wrapped around her,

her eyes glistening with the onset of tears. She shook her head. She was smart enough to know that what was coming was coming and that giving trouble would certainly get her trouble.

"W,what do you want?" she whispered nervously.

"Oh, we'll get to that," Draco replied. "But first things first." He pointed at her robe with the knife.

Amy looked around timidly and then untied the sash to her robe. She then let the robe slip from her shoulders letting it slide down her arms. She removed it and held it in her hands before her, a futile attempt to cover up.

"Just toss it on the couch, Amy, that's a good girl." Draco ordered. He had a real way about him. His voice was smooth and friendly, but with a cutting edge, like the stiletto he held in his hand.

Once the robe was tossed away, Amy's delights were more readily appreciated. Her legs were long and toned, slightly muscular. Her skin was pale. Goosebumps ran up and down her arms. The nightie, reaching down to just below the tops of her thighs, was translucent, giving a greenish tint to her skin beneath it. Her breasts, although veiled, revealed their shape and size readily. They quivered slightly, not large, but certainly ample. Her bush below was dark.

"Oh, Amy, you're not a natural blonde. What a shame," Draco teased her. I could see Remo, behind the girl casting an appreciative leer at the globes of her ass. You could tell what he liked.

The girl's tears were flowing freely now, staining her face. Whatever was going to happen was certainly not going to be to her liking. How far would we go, what was really happening here? Was she going to die? I could sense her mind clicking away. Her lips were pulled tensely shut.

Meanwhile, I thought, what was Genda up to? As if in

answer to my thoughts, Genda's face appeared from behind the corner of the hallway. His head nodded to his side, beckoning. Draco looked at me and I got the message. I stepped quietly from the room and followed him.

We went down a short a short flight of stairs which led to a long hallway. Genda signaled me to be quiet and I followed him to the third doorway along the passage. As we approached I could hear moaning, a woman's voice. A familiar sound. Someone was getting it on.

We crept quietly to the doorway and I peered into the room through the slightly opened door. There was a large double bed in the center of the room, framed by ornate posts. On top of the bed I could see a female posterior hunched over, naked and gyrating slowly. A little further towards the head of the bed was another woman, long dark hair, slender of face, her eyes shut, grimacing in passion. Her legs were spread widely. The moans were coming from her. Well someone was having the breakfast of champions here. It looked like we were going to get a little bonus from our trip.

Genda pushed the doorway open slowly. Everything was going fine until it creaked. The action on the bed stopped suddenly. A tussled, blond head peered out from behind the bare ass, the brunette's eyes jumped open. Surprise!

Genda and I stepped quickly into the room. The yodeler jumped up from the bed, as quick a reaction as I've ever seen. Pulling the comforter from the bed she tossed it into the air and sprang towards the screened doorway which led to a porch outside. She burst right through the screen.

Meanwhile, Genda was struggling to push the comforter off of his head. The brunette was frozen in shock, the opposite of her quicksilver lover. I clicked open my pig sticker and crept towards her menacingly. Genda shot out the door after the Flash.

The brunette crawled backwards on the bed, until her back was flush against the headboard. She was, of course, naked so I could see her deeply tanned body. Her breasts were small and pert, white and pale, the nipples hard, surrounded by dark and wide areolas. Her hands were pushing down on the bed as if to give her purchase in pushing the bed frame through the wall behind her. Seeing that Genda was in hot pursuit of the muff muncher, I took matters into my own hands, so to speak.

"I'm only going to tell you once what I want you to do. If you give me trouble, I'll stick you where it will hurt a lot. Got that?" The girl nodded frantically. "Now I want you to lie down on the bed, face down, towards me. Then you are going to put your hands behind your back. Any noise out of you and you'll have some holes in hose pretty little tits of yours. Ok?" She nodded again.

She nervously crept forward on the bed and lay down with her head towards me. Her moans had now turned to a little mewing whine. Just once, she stole a look at the open doorway, the screen burst out. I measured just how big a leap I would have to make to catch her, having foolishly approached from the wrong side of the bed. What a picture that would make, me and Genda chasing naked girls through the woods. Kind of like satyrs in the old Greek myths. Draco would not be amused.

Fear getting the better part of her, the brunette complied with my instructions, laying her long, thin body before me, placing her hands behind her back. Her delicate fingers twitched nervously in anticipation for what she surely knew would come next. Not wanting to disappoint, I pulled a long leather thong from my jacket pocket. Always good to be prepared. I knelt on the edge of the bed and swung my leg over the girl's legs, pinning them beneath me. Putting the knife in my mouth, pirate style, I crossed her wrists and then tied them tightly with the leather strap, once up and down, once across and then back again. Nice and tight, but leaving a little room for circulation. Didn't want these long, twitching fingers to fall off, did I?

After securing her arms, I turned towards her legs. Enough running for today, I thought. I pulled another, longer strap from my pocket and addressed the girl's ankles. I tied one end on her left leg and the other on her right, leaving about a foot and a half between them. I didn't want to have to carry her after all.

I paused for a moment, taking in my fine work. Her legs were warm beneath me and I could feel her squirm with discomfort. I ran my hands down her legs, a familiar feeling stirring in my groin. "Mmmm," I thought, "delightful. Why not knock off a little piece right here?" Well, if I wanted to die today I could do that. But maybe I'd just live a little longer.

Discretion having won over ardor, I moved off of the bed and pulled the girl's legs after me. My knife now back in my hand, I grabbed her arm with my free one and stood her up. She stood about 5'9", a couple of inches below my nose. It was good to be tall. Her breathing was quick and shallow as she stared into my face, fearing what would come next. I glanced around the room and saw a pair of little pink panties at my feet. Just what I needed. Reaching down without letting go of the girl's arm I swept them off of the floor with the tip of my knife.

"Now, open you mouth honey, I have a little present for you."

The girl looked with horror at the panties and then back at me. "We don't want you making a lot of noise, dearie, so we have to shut you up. You've been good so far so let's just keep this friendly."

Naked, surprised in an act of deviate sexual abandon, arms trussed behind her and a 7" slip of steel inches from her face, I guess the girl thought she might as well go with the program. She opened her mouth slowly, still mewing, her knees trembling. My rapier having done its duty, I clicked it closed and addressed the problem at hand. I stood right up to her, her breasts squeezed against my chest. Scrunching the panties into a, little wad, I held the back of her head and stuffed them into her mouth. Now cooperation is a relative term and she had opened her mouth a wee bit in response to my directive, but not enough for my concerns. It was with a little effort that I was able to wedge the panties inside. I must say, the brunette looked quite forlorn. Oh, well, you can't please everybody.

I couldn't resist a little feel and so I messaged first one, then the other of her enticing mounds. They were a little larger than they had first appeared, probably because she had been hunching her shoulders to back away from me, each one a little more than a handful. Soft and firm, hot to the touch, her breasts heaved as she fought for air behind the mouthful of panties. She just stared at me in fright. Not what she had been thinking about a few moments ago. I was sure she liked it when Blondie rubbed her tits. She probably moaned and cooed with delight. But not now. All I got was mewing and whimpering. Well, enough fun, I mean Genda was outside somewhere running down the muff diver and Draco would want to know what I was up to. Back to work.

Grabbing her arm I tugged my pretty captive towards the door of the bedroom. Once in the hallway I had her lie on the floor while I double-checked the rest of the rooms. Two other bedrooms and a bath. No one home. I stepped back into the hallway and assisted the girl back to her feet. As we approached the stairs I could see a little problem. A foot and a half was enough for walking, albeit little baby steps, but not enough to manage the steps to the main floor. Was I going to do some heavy lifting after all? Shit.

I gave in to necessity and, after spinning the girl to face me, shoved my shoulder into her gut and lifted her up. She bent in half complacently avoiding what could have been a nasty bump on the head. I carried her up the stairs into the hallway and around the corner into the den.

Draco was sitting comfortably in one of the easy chairs. A small pile of delicate green fabric lay in the center of the room. The girl, Amy, was nowhere to be seen. Neither was Remo.

"Where's Genda?" Draco spat.

"He's chasing down an Amazon," I said as I eased my burden to the floor.

"What the fuck happened?"

"We caught this one and her girlfriend en flagrente delicto downstairs, but her girlfriend threw herself through a screen door and took off. Genda took off after her."

"Fuck! What a mess! Are you guys clowns or what?

"She was fast, she…"

"Go help him for Christ's sake. If she gets away we gotta book out of here."

I was about to comply when I heard a commotion at the front door. I heard it swing open, banging against the doorstop, and the sound of boots striking the hardwood floor. Genda appeared around the corner. He had the Amazon in tow. Saved by the bell!

Genda dragged his burden into the room causing her to stumble down the short steps. He had her by her bushy blonde hair, and, ignoring her muffled cries of alarm, dragged her to the center of the room. Her arms were pinioned behind her back, tethered high up with a lead going around her throat. Not good for the maintenance of a beneficial oxygen supply. Her body was covered with scratches, blood oozing here and there. Genda had jammed a short, thick branch between her teeth and secured it tightly behind her head. "This bitch bit me," was all he said.

Draco looked thoughtfully at the bleeding blonde. "Well, don't let her strangle. Truss her up and we'll get down to business here."

Genda shrugged. He pulled the girl to her knees and released the bonds around her neck. He pushed her to the floor and secured one end of a leather thong to her ankle. Looking around dumbly, he seemed lost for a moment. Then looking up, he got a bright idea.

He lifted the girl from the floor by one ankle as if she were a featherweight and tossed the free end of the thong over the beam which ran across the middle of the room. Holding the thong's end in one hand he reached out and grabbed the other ankle. Deftly, he circled the other ankle with the thong and tied it off. Blondie was strung up, upside down with her head barely touching the floor. She was going nowhere.

In the meantime, the brunette was taking this all in. Her mewing had not stopped. Genda turned to her in annoyance. "Shut the fuck up!" he roared. The girl mewed all the more. Genda pushed her to the floor and untied one of her ankles. In a moment she was hanging upside down next to her partner.

Just then, Remo returned to the room with little Amy in front of him. She was naked, of course, and she was carrying a small tray with a coffee pot, some cups, a sugar bowl and a small pitcher of milk. Spoons rattled on the tray as she walked. Her face collapsed into a grimace as she saw her friends hanging bottoms up.

"I see you have some friends over, Amy. Anyone else 'hanging around?'" Draco enquired.

The tray started to shake a little more.

"Maybe we'll take another look around, OK? Remo, check out the upstairs."

Remo darted away. Genda followed him. "Coffee, Harry?" Draco asked.

"Sure, a little milk please."

Amy placed the clattering tray on the table before the couch. She was sobbing silently. Awkwardly she poured two cups of coffee and placed a dollop of milk in one, a little sugar in the other. Draco had apparently already placed his order.

Picking up the cups, she handed one to me and turned to give one to Draco. The cup was shaking visibly in her hand. "Now, don't spill it Amy. A good hostess takes care of her guests, doesn't she? If you got coffee on my new pants I would be quite upset."

Amy stepped carefully over to Draco and offered the cup to him. He took it.

As she backed away from him, her sobbing became heavier and louder. Something was up. Was there someone else in the house? Someone she hoped would get away?

Draco motioned to the girl and she slipped quickly to her knees. Without instruction, she placed her hands behind her head. I saw that Draco had begun her training already.

We sat sipping our coffee for a few moments contemplating Amy's delightful form. Her breasts jutted out nicely, pale circles around her nipples, maybe just an ounce of fat around her middle. Her knees were wide, as they should be, and her cunt lips peaked just beyond the dark bush of hair surrounding them. She did look good as a blonde. Perhaps a little work with a razor was in order. Without pussy hair, only her hairdresser would know for sure.

The tread of boots in the hallway signaled the return of the Mau Maus. Surprise, surprise, a little, naked, dark haired girl was walking between them. Remo had her by the hand. She was a little, bony girl, black hair behind her head in a pony tail. Her lips were trembling, as was natural in these circumstances, her head down. Remo led her into the room.

"She was hiding in a closet," he said, releasing her as he pulled her into the room. The momentum carried her close to Amy. Amy's sobbing increased, just below hysterical.

"Now, Amy, who is this, someone special?" Draco asked. "You shouldn't have hidden her from us. We're all friends here. Please introduce me."

Amy was in no shape for a conversation, but managed to spit out two words, "M,my sister." Okay, almost three words.

"Ah, how delightful," Draco exclaimed, "a sister act."

"N,no, please," Amy sputtered, "please, please don't hurt her. Please let us go. I'll tell you anything you want. Please don't hurt us!" Amy was reaching into quite deep reserves for this.

"Well, we'll see what happens, Amy. Lets first calm down and have a little chat. It if makes you feel any better, we're not going to kill you. You and your friends are much too lovely for that." Draco turned to the younger girl, "What's you're name little one?"

"Robin," she whispered quietly, her head still bowed, too frightened to look up. She wore nothing but her pony tail holder as Remo and Genda had apparently relieved her of clothing before bringing her downstairs. She looked around eighteen. Her breasts were small and pointed. Her legs were slender, her hips wide. There was a small tattoo on her stomach just above her pubic hair. A butterfly.

"Now, Robin, I want you to sit on my lap as I talk to your sister, be a good girl and come over here."

Robin glanced sidelong at her sister and then stepped slowly to Draco. As she got close he grabbed her arm and pulled her onto his lap. She was tiny but Draco was no giant either. She fit there nicely.

Draco wrapped one arm around her shoulders and ran his other hand over her belly and then down her leg. She shivered at his touch but made no resistance. "You're a pretty little thing, aren't you Robin. Do you have a boyfriend? Would you like to be my girlfriend, Robin?" He was teasing her. He slid his thigh between her legs opening her for better access. Her arms were pressed behind her by Draco's right arm and left shoulder. He caressed her right breast. "Very nice little tits, Robin," he said. "If you would like, I'll suck on them for you, would you like that?"

Robin responded with a soft and quiet "No."

"Oh, that's too bad, Robin, because I really like to suck on soft little tits like yours. Maybe if I give you a little encouragement you'll feel more like it." Draco ran his hand between her thighs, first pulling gently on the thin, wiry hairs which covered the girl's sex and then probing deeper. Robin gave out a little squeak as Draco pushed his fingers past the entrance. He then turned to Amy, still sobbing quietly, kneeling before him, displaying her tantalizing charms.

"Ok now, Amy, do you think Dougie will be back soon?"

"I,I don't know."

"Well, what do you know, Amy?"

"I don't know where he went. He goes out a lot."

"Business, I suppose, huh Amy?"

"Y,yes, I think so." Amy stared down at the floor, not bearing to see her little sister's abuse.

"Dougie owes us a lot of money, Amy, and we're a little pissed at him as you can tell. Is there any money here in the house?

"Yes."

"Where?"

"In the bedroom upstairs. There's a small safe." Amy was thinking, "Maybe if I give them the money, maybe we'll be ok. Maybe they won't hurt us. Maybe, oh maybe they'll let us go." This glimmer of hope had given her a bit more confidence. Well, maybe she was wrong.

Remo stood watching Amy's ass, which he surely desired a piece of. Genda, meanwhile was more interested in the brunette the blonde had been gemauching downstairs. He had spread her knees as she hung upside down and was eyeing her snatch with undisguised lust. He glanced back at Draco who gave a slight shrug as if to say, "Ok, dive in." Genda needed no further encouragement as he buried his face between the brunette's legs. She began to mew again. The blonde looked on silently. She was biding her time. She would be ready to take her chance to get out of this if she got it. She had some real fun waiting for her.

Draco continued with Amy, his hand now nestled well into Robin's quim. Her eyes were closed, her face in a grimace. "OK, Amy, why don't you show Harry and Remo here where the safe is and get the money, Ok?"

Amy nodded yes and then glancing back and forth at Remo and me, slowly got to her feet. She kept her hands behind her head.

"Remo, I think we need a little leash on Amy here, we don't want her to feel insecure, now do we?" I asked.

He grunted and pulled a thong from his pocket. He tightened it quickly around Amy's neck. He tugged on it slightly and she moved to go upstairs. I followed.

Remo was in heaven as the girl's ass jiggled softly as she mounted the stairs. He let her have enough lead to get her ass almost at eye level. I couldn't see his face, but I was sure he was licking his chops. Sooner or later, Amy would have to spread her fine white cheeks for him and get her fill of Mau Mau cock. Maybe sooner rather than later. I thought not sooner since we surely couldn't hang around here all day. But once we got back to the house, well, who knows then.

Amy led us into a large well appointed bedroom, obviously the master suite. Just a short while ago she was lying here maybe dreaming of her fine man and aching for his return. Maybe she was dreaming of making long and passionate love amid the pile of dough he would bring back with him. She might have contemplated giving him a long, tender blowjob as a reward for a job well done. But maybe not. I was fun to think about it though.

We followed Amy to a picture on the wall, a small oil painting of a Dutch country scene. Children were romping around a maypole, cows and chickens galore, big cottony clouds overhead. A young woman and a man were standing in a doorway to a little cottage, embracing. Home sweet home. I don't know much about art, but it looked like an original. Probably cost a pretty penny. I bet that Amy picked it out, her ultimate plans for her and Dougie reflected in the homely scene. I wonder what Dougie thought.

The picture was hinged to the wall and Amy pulled it open. A small combination safe was there. With a quick look over her shoulder, Amy turned back and, with a few deft turns, the safe opened. Remo pulled her away. I looked in and, sitting atop a small pile of cash was a small pistol, a Beretta. Tsk, tsk, tsk. Was Amy trying a fast one?

Remo lashed out and slapped Amy across the face. The force of the blow drove her back and she fell onto the bed. Remo was on top of her in an instant, pulling her up by her hair and then tossing her face down on the bed. He clamped her arms together and held her wrists with one of his meaty oversized hands.

"De little girl is bad, Harry. She wants to shoot us. What we done, eh?" Remo wasn't mad, he was just enjoying his opportunity to manhandle Amy.

"Get the stuff out, Harry, let's see what we got."

I looked back into the safe and placed the Berretta in my jacket pocket. I then pulled out the cash. Maybe twenty thousand. A few jewels were at the back, a necklace, some rings and a bracelet. I gathered them and turned to get a pillowcase from the bed. Remo had taken the opportunity to introduce himself to Amy's ass. He had spread her legs and was stroking her bush while jamming his thumb up her behind. Amy was crying and moaning, her voice muffled by the bedclothes. Well, you had to give her credit for trying.

"Ok Amy, where's the rest," I said as I dropped the swag into a pillow case.

"In the closet, in the closet!" she called out, "Please get him off me, please."

"Now Amy, I don't control what Remo does, but if we can get the rest of the dough and get back downstairs, I'm sure Mr. Draco will calm Remo down. So where in the closet?"

"In the ceiling, there's a loose tile. Push it back and there's a strongbox. That's all that's here, I swear."

"Ok, but if you're lying, I'll ask Remo here to finish the job he's starting."

"No, I swear, I swear!"

I walked over to the large walk-in closet and flipped on the light. It had gotten a lot lighter since the forty minutes or so we had been here but I still needed the light to see my way. I pushed up on the ceiling tiles and found one to be looser than the others. Pushing it up, I stepped on my toes to reach above the doorframe. Sure enough, there was a strongbox there. I pulled it over to the opening where the tile had been and brought it down. It wasn't locked. I mean what was the sense in locking something that could be carried away? I brought the strongbox over to the bed.

Amy was squirming and whining in pain as Remo now had the better part of three fingers up her ass. She would learn to take more down the road.

I opened the box and low and behold, three or four neat stacks of cash. All 100's, all neatly bound into thousand dollar bundles. I counted thirty five.

"Is this it, Amy?"

"Yes, yes, please!"

"It's not going to make my boss very happy. Dougie owes a lot more than this, and with interest and collection expenses added, well, this is just a drop in the bucket. Are you sure there's no more?"

"Yes, I'm sure. I don't know where he keeps the rest of the money. It's not in the house, it's somewhere else. He hides it. Please, please, make him stop!"

"Remo, I think we'd better get downstairs and give Mr. Draco the bad news, don't you?"

"What you say, Harry, I'll save my fun for later. OK chickie?" He gave Amy a little push in her back. "I said 'OK chickie'?" he repeated, pushing her a little harder.

"Ok! Ok! Please let me up, please!"

Remo stood up and pulled Amy to her feet by the tether around her neck. Her hands went to her throat as she gagged.

"Hands behind head dearie, like we showed you." Amy complied and the pressure on her throat diminished. "Let's go." He gave her a little push to the door.

Downstairs, the scene had changed slightly from when we left. Robin was on the floor, her hands tied behind her, hogtied to her ankles. The brunette was beside her in a similar tie. The blonde was still hanging upside down, but the stick in her mouth had been replaced by duct tape across her lips. Genda was placing a small black bag over her head, pulling it tight by a draw string. We were getting ready to go.

"This is all we could get," I told Draco as we entered the room, Amy preceding us. I showed him the fifty five thousand and the jewelry. Draco frowned at Amy.

"Well Amy, I'm afraid we're going to collect you and you friends here as collateral. When Dougie gets home, he'll see our little calling card and know what to do. Maybe we can still work things out, but he'll have to hurry. Now I have a little tape recorder here and you're going to leave him a little message. You will tell him that some friends came by and that you all decided to go on a little trip with us. He can contact us in the usual way and we'll have a little chat. OK?"

Amy began to cry again. "Oh please mister, we don't have anything. I'll do what ever you want, just don't kidnap us. You can fuck me if you want, I'll do whatever you want, just please don't take us away."

"Now, Amy, do you think that we came all this was for a little fuck?" Draco's voice was hard edged now, menacing. "You need to do what you're told, understand? We could hurt you terribly if we wanted to, maybe hurt little Robin here. Do you want that? Let's just get with the program now, OK?" His voice returned to its normal tone. Pleasing, but firm. Real firm.

Amy nodded affirmatively, the fear clear in her eyes. She knelt down at Remo's urging. Draco held the recorder to her mouth and turned it on. Amy's voice was tiny, pleading, quivering.

"Doug," she hesitated, looking up at Draco. He urged her on. "Some people came here, they took us somewhere. They want you to call them. Please Doug, please…." She was about to say more when Draco shut off the recorder. He popped out the tape and placed it on the end table. He nodded to Remo.

Remo quickly flew up the steps and out the front door. Draco turned to Amy and motioned for her to lie on the floor. Sobbing, she complied and lay down next to her sister. Robin and the unnamed brunette were whimpering. Their lips too had been taped but they could hear pretty good I was sure. Draco took another length of leather and fastened Amy's arms behind her. He then tied her ankles together leaving a short lead as I had previously done with the brunette. He motioned to me and I released the other girls from their hog ties and fastened their ankles likewise.

Genda approached the blonde who had given him so much trouble. He pulled the black bag from her head. She looked up at him with hatred. Not an ounce of fear in this broad. Genda leaned over and looked her in the face. "Ready to travel, bitch?" he said. He then gave her a short sharp punch in her solar plexus. The woman's eyes clamped shut and she gasped for breath. Genda quickly released her ankles from the beam and dropped her down on the floor. Her body landed with a loud thump. He fastened her ankles closely, no walking for her. He put the bag back on.

I could hear the van pull up to the garage below us and Draco motioned me to get the girls up from the floor. First Robin, then Amy. Genda stood the brunette to her feet. More black bags completed the preparation and we led the girls one by one down the basement stairs to the garage. When we were finished, Amy, Robin and the brunette were carefully stashed in the van, lashed feet and head to rings in the van floor. As I went to go back upstairs to help Genda with the blonde, I could hear a thumping down the steps. Genda was dragging the blonde down the stairs, her feet in his arms, her head striking each step as she descended. Genda smiled at me. "This bitch bit me." That was all he said. He pulled her into the van, secured her to the floor and then got into the front seat with Remo. Draco and I spread a tarp over the naked foursome, clipping its corners down so that only a series of rough bulges showed underneath. Not much of a cover, perhaps, but just enough to let Remo or Genda to put a slug or two into any nosey cops.

The van pulled away. Draco and I followed on foot walking down the driveway to the Caddy. Draco paused to light a cigar. It was about 6:30. Our whole escapade had taken about one and a half hours. We were fifty five thousand and four broads to the better, or at least Klitzman was. He would get the rest of the dough and Dougie too, I was sure of that.

## CHAPTER EIGHT
## MARA IS TAUGHT A THING OR TWO

When I awoke I was alone. No longer confined in my coffin, I was unbound, still naked and lying on a cot. As my eyes became focused I looked about to gain my bearings. The room was small, the walls and ceiling white, the floor, carpeted in a light blue. My head hurt like a demon had passed through it. Groggily I sat up, pushing my feet off of the cot and onto the floor. I was amazed at my relative freedom. Even the crude collar which Nicky had placed around my neck was gone. I couldn't believe I could actually open my eyes at will, touch my body, open my mouth. My jaw ached from the days of confinement, my legs and arms stiff. Someone had obviously washed me while I was out, my body smelled clean and my hair, for the first time since my imprisonment, soft and fresh.

I saw a pitcher of water on a table next to me with a small glass next to it. I wondered briefly if it was drugged, but drank anyway. If they wanted me drugged, they didn't need any tricks. I had no power to stop them if that was what they wanted.

I lay back down and must have slept some more. I awoke when the door opened and a thin, dark skinned man, about thirty, entered pushing a small hospital cart before him. He looked at me nonchalantly as he pushed the cart over to where I sat. I was, of course, still naked, and they had not provided any coverings to the bed. I crossed my legs reflexively and crossed my arms in front of my breasts. For a short while I had felt almost comfortable about being in this room, safe again, maybe brought back to sanity, to a world where I was a person. But here I was again, naked, about to be the subject of some act or acts by this strange man. I huddled away from him into the corner of the bed.

"This is a medical exam," the man said calmly. "You have nothing to worry from me as long as you cooperate." His voice was inflected with a Caribbean lilt. His hair black, a small goatee surrounding his mouth. "If you fail to cooperate I will call in the guard and you will be forced to cooperate and then be punished. Do you understand?" I nodded yes.

The man proceeded to examine me, looking into my eyes, my ears, feeling my pulse, taking my blood pressure, everything my regular doctor would have done. I followed his directions meekly, without questions. He had spoken of a punishment. I dreaded the thought of what my captors could do to me. Whoever they were, whatever they wanted from me they were certainly people to be feared.

The orderly proceeded to measure my body, my wrists and neck, my ankles. He felt my breasts, for lumps I supposed, but also measured them for circumference, size, the distance from my nipples to my neck. He also measured my legs, their length and width, the size of my vagina, the distance between there and my anus. He probed them both with a gloved hand, causing me to gasp and squirm. He drew blood, took my saliva and vaginal secretions and a urine sample. He even took a small scale from the cart and weighed me. All the time he was silent except for his commands to turn, lift a leg, present my breasts to him. Finally, when he was done he took several pictures of me, side views and front, my breasts and between my legs, my body framed by the whiteness of the walls. When he was done he offered me a slight smile and, using a key on a chain from his belt, opened the door and left.

About a half hour later some food arrived. A bowl of fruit, a small chicken filet, more water. It was delivered by another man, still dark, a golden earring through his right ear. He dropped the tray on the table next to the cot. His smile didn't seem half as friendly as the medical technician's. "Eat" was all he said and left.

I wasn't very hungry. I remembered the words spoken to me by Nicky in the car, by Draco. I was to be trained, opened they said. Enslaved. Was this what it felt to be enslaved, to be an object? What was next? What awaited me? I was soon to learn.

I had finished the fruit and chicken when the door burst open again. It was the man who had delivered the food. He stepped forward to claim the food tray and, glancing over his shoulder, nodded to someone behind him. As he stepped from the room a large black man, tall, broad shoulders, wearing a bright red t-shirt and loose, tan, canvas pants stepped into the room. He had two words for me: "Get up."

Cringing, I stepped up from the cot. He grabbed my arm and pulled me away to the center of the room. The room seemed even smaller with this giant looming over me. His hand around my wrist was like a vise, his fingers easily circling it. He carried a small black bag which he placed on the floor in front of him. Reaching in, he pulled out several leather and steel objects. Looking at them, I knew they were for me. My body chilled with fear. Was this the moment I had been dreading? Could I negotiate, tell them I'd changed my mind, that I wanted to leave, that the game was over? Looking at this hulk before me I was sure I could not.

"P-please, don't hurt me," was all I could squeak out, my throat was constricted, my knees weak with fear.

"Turn around," was all he replied.

I did what I was told, circling to my left, not wanting to let him leave my sight, fearing the untelegraphed blow, the unforwarned act. He roughly pulled my hair up off of my shoulders and I felt something snap shut around my neck. I reached up with my hands to feel a collar around my neck, thick, made of leather, with rings. I felt a belt wrapped around my waist, snugly clasped behind me, clicking closed. He then grabbed my right hand and spun me around, locking a bracelet to my right and then my left wrist. There could be no confusion about what these were for: my training, my enslavement.

I was pushed towards the cot, my wrists having been clipped to rings on the belt, slightly behind my back. I fell back and felt my legs being lifted, separated. I closed my eyes, fearing the worst, only to feel my ankles being encircled with the same leather bonds as were around my wrists. The man pulled me back to my feet. Holding my head still by the hair with one hand, he bent over and reached back into the bag on the floor. As he did, he caused my body to bend over with him, my head pulled down. I squealed in pain. As he straightened up he looked at me with a seeming perplexed look. He looked at his other hand and remembering his next task pulled my head back and plunged a gag into my mouth. This was no ball gag, but a long thick plug shaped like a cock mounted on a leather base which covered my mouth and chin. He pulled it painfully tight.

I was bound, confined, trussed up for use. I knew it. I wanted to scream, but couldn't. I wanted to fight off this hulk, to punch and scratch him, but this too was forlorn. The giant didn't wait for me to gain my equilibrium, he pulled me to the wall across from the door and, using a ring on the outside of the gag, chained me to a hook about a foot above my head. The effect was to pull my head backwards and up, giving me a view of the ceiling and little else. My back was to the door and my captor. After affixing me, the man stood there admiring his handiwork. I felt his hands descending my back, feeling the globes of my rear end, circling in front of me and grabbing my breasts. I could feel him press close to me. He leaned over and whispered in my ear.

"Soon we will dance, little one. Very soon." He left. He turned out the light.

An hour, two, I don't know for sure, went by. I swayed gently at my bonds, my neck aching, my jaw pulled up. I couldn't ignore the feel of the cock-gag in my mouth. Was this what Nicky wanted for me? Did he know what was happening to me? Would I ever see him again? The darkness served as a cloak and a comfort in a way. The trappings of my enslavement, my collar and other bonds, could fade away in the darkness. I could pretend, as strange as that may seem, even momentarily, that this was not happening to me, but was a dream, a nightmare, part of the dark which would vanish when light once more was let back into my life. That my nightmare was in fact real would soon be made very clear to me.

The door flew open again without warning and the room was filled with light. I felt my head being released and I was pulled by the chain affixed to my gag out of the room and into the hallway outside. Two other women stood in the hallway, bound and gagged as I was. With them was the young girl from the cellar, the one whose eyes had haunted me in my imprisonment. The women were lined up, one behind the other, the chains from their gags affixed to the collar of the female in front of them. They were, as was I, naked.

The lead woman was affixed to my collar and we were pulled down the narrow hallway. Door after door was passed. We stopped at two more to recover the inhabitants for our forced march. Did all of these rooms hold women awaiting their fate? How and why did these other women get selected for this trip? I knew that all of these women could not have been brought here willingly and I began to understand the depth of the trouble I had let myself in for. Slaves, slavers, could this really be, here in the twenty first century?

We were led through another door, down a dark hallway and up a small set of stairs. We entered a large room, large overstuffed furniture, sofas and chairs against the walls, a plush red rug. Six chains descended from the ceiling in the middle of the room. These, I knew, were for us.

We were each affixed by the rings on our gags to the chains from the ceiling. The chains were pulled tight enough to elevate our heads slightly. Our legs were chained together, left to right, causing our legs to spread. We were displayed.

As we stood bound and silent, the room began to fill with activity. A large divan was pulled out in front of us, some drinks were brought in, chairs pulled from the walls. The men who circulated through the room, all dressed in red shirts and canvas pants, would stop on occasion and admire the showcase of flesh before them. More than once a mouth fastened on one of my nipples, or a finger explored my sex, gently rubbing until, lubricated, it could penetrate. I saw some women enter the room as well, two slender, dark haired women, dressed in flowing skirts, bodices that reached up to the tips of their breasts. They wore collars on their necks, and, around the wrists, the same bracelets we wore.

Suddenly the room snapped to attention, the men around the room stopped their meandering, the serving women knelt on either side of a large stuffed chair that had been placed before us. In walked a thin man, slight of build, but carrying himself with the air of command, a self assured authority. He strolled to the chair before us and sat himself in it, his hands wandering to heads and chins of the women kneeling at his sides. The room was silent. The lights went down except for small spot lights which shown directly on the six of us, displayed, proffered for this cruel looking man's intentions, whatever they were tonight.

After taking us in from afar he stood and approached. Standing next to him was a handsome, dark haired woman, about thirty five, tall, with gleaming black eyes. She deferred to the man before us, but, collarless, dressed in a dark floor length gown, she clearly had some special role to play, not a slave, a mistress.

The man walked slowly down the line of women. Feeling, pinching, caressing. It was clear that our faces, our visages were of little interest to him. Our bodies, our breasts, the curve of our hips the strength of our thighs, these were what he sought to know. And most importantly, our responsiveness, the feel of our loins.

He chatted amiably with the woman, discussing the charms of the women he passed, she apparently telling him something about them, their age, their lineage, their names. As they reached me, the woman spoke quietly to the Man. "Mr. Diskare, this one is from Mr. Krikorios, for training. She enslaved herself to him at his request. I offered to train her myself since Mr. Krikorian is a special friend of our friend."

"Yes, yes, I agree. You shall have her, initially anyway. I want Nicky to be especially satisfied," he said, looking at me, his hand on my sex, probing, penetrating. My fear and anxiety made me tremble at his touch. I felt the fire within me warming. I despised myself for it. I knew the whole room was watching me. His eyes bore down on me, fixating me as he probed deeper and deeper. My breath was rising, I could feel the flush of my skin.

"I see that Nicky has made a very good choice. She seems quite passionate," he told the woman.

Just as my passion had begun to rise, despite myself, he released me. I struggled to gain my breath. The woman smiled at me, reached out and stroked the side of my head, my hair. "Oh, yes, she will be exciting to train," she replied. Her voice was smooth as silk, deep, with a slight edge that carried a hint of her inner cruelty. "I will enforce a very strict regimen for her," she added.

I could feel the fear climb from the pit of my stomach through my chest and down my arms, chills, trembling, sweating, my palms hot and wet. I knew I should fear this woman. She had cruelty written into her brow. What demon ate at her, I never knew, nor, did she, I think. But I could see it reflected in her eyes, the hollowness there, the lack of warmth, the deadliness of her smile.

The man she called Diskare walked further down the line, the woman following him, slowly, like an acolyte. He stopped before the young girl at the end of the string. Although my head was slightly lifted, I could see him reach out and caress her tiny breasts.

"A little token from Estelle I see, Carla. She is going to spoil you."

Carla, replied, "Well she knows that she will always be welcome when she visits us. She likes to keep me happy. I know she's done well by you, Mr. Diskare." Her tone was respectful, deferential.

"Oh, yes, very well indeed. But still, I'm sure you won't mind if I taste this little morsel tonight, do you. I'll try not to damage her."

"Not at all, I think breaking the little ones in right away is the best thing to do. They adapt so well afterwards."

Diskare stood back now from the half dozen women strung in front of him like so many paper dolls. "Ladies," he clearly wanted our attention, "welcome to our little island." His smile, cold as ice, deadly. An attendant handed him a riding crop. This was a man to listen to.

"You have all come here to begin a new life. You no doubt have been wondering about your fate ever since a gag was first slipped over your face, or a binding applied to your wrists." He stroked the face of the woman next to me with the riding crop. Her eyes were wide with fear.

"I must speak plainly and directly. You have been selected to serve as slaves. You have forever lost the right to control your own lives, your actions, your bodies. You are displayed here now before me as what you are now, the property of others. You are persons no longer, although you do have physical value. You are all very attractive and, apparently, responsive females. Your value will improve with training no doubt. But do not think for one minute that this value can accrue to your benefit in any way. For what would be the point of granting rights to a chattel, a horse, a dog, or," he paused while he tapped the woman's breasts with the riding crop, "a cow?" He paused to let the force of what he had said sink in. My mind was screaming with protest, remorse, terror. I was so frightened that I felt a trickle of pee roll down my leg. I had lost control of myself.

Diskare continued, "Tonight, you will begin your training. You will learn to serve and obey. That will be your guiding light. You will spread your legs, open your mouths, offer your backsides, to be penetrated, possessed, by those who might desire you. No part of you remains yours. You will shortly feel the kiss of the lash across your breasts, your bellies, your thighs. This is to bring home to you your powerlessness, your abjectivity. Get used to it; it will be part of your daily lives. And if for any reason, you fail in your training or your duties, or, from time to time, for no reason at all, you will be punished, severely, cruelly.

"Those of you who respond well to training can expect some pleasure of your own, as we will reward the sensuous and obedient among you. But remember, at any time, your very lives, your very existence belongs to your masters who may take it with no less thought than you might put down an unruly dog or an annoying pet.

"The rules of the house are simple. You will open yourself at any time to anyone who desires you, and pleasure them in any way they desire. You will remain silent except to cry out in pleasure or pain, or, in those limited circumstances when you are directed to speak. You will never touch yourselves or anyone else without the permission of your masters. You will care for our property, your physical selves, as instructed."

All during this little speech, the man called Diskare strolled slowly up and down the line of women before him. All eyes were on him and ears pricked up, keyed into his voice. An answer, finally an answer to the question which had become an obsession to me during the last few days, and I am sure to these women, posed and displayed as I was: "What was happening, what was to become of me?"

I was coming to realize the scale of the forces Nicky had induced me to surrender to. We six women and the others who had been there in the cellar with us but had gone to fates as yet unknown to me, had been collected, stored and shipped to a far away place, across national boundaries and, necessarily, across rivers and an ocean, efficiently and apparently without fear of consequence.

What remained for me to learn was whether I belonged to Nicky or to this "organization". Nicky was my master, I assumed, since I had surrendered myself to him, something that I now bitterly regretted. These other women, what had brought them here? I could only deduce, correctly as it turned out, that these women had not volunteered themselves to slavery as I had, that they had been kidnapped, whisked away from their lives without consent, without any inkling of what was in store for them. It was bad enough to have to blame myself for foolishness, a tragic mistake, but these women were totally innocent. Their demise, their enslavement, was an act of fate, sparked, do doubt, by the very voluptuousness and beauty they had sought after, fostered and treasured in their former lives.

But their presence spoke volumes for the power of this organization. Not only did it have the ability to select out almost a dozen beautiful women, abduct them and remove them to a foreign shore, but also it had a use for them, a market. To be in a position to obtain value for them they had to be in a position of power to protect themselves, but also to protect their clients. For how else could the ultimate users of these "chattels", these objects of desire, be convinced to involve themselves in what amounted to international piracy? Protection from their crimes was obviously a major part of the enticement to participate in this modern version of this most ancient institution. The organization and its clients had little or nothing to fear from lawful authority. No government's writ ran here.

Diskare paced back and forth as he spoke to us, taking in the dangling display before him. The chains which ran from the ceiling to our gags elevated our heads just enough for discomfort and to ensure erect posture, but not enough so that we could not follow him with our eyes. Finally he stopped before the woman to my right, a pale, slender blonde. He stepped forward so that his face was inches away from hers. His hand dropped below her waist and from the moans and whimpers she commenced, it was clear that he was forcing his way into her sex.

She was tall, with long legs, but her spread stance brought her down to slightly above Diskare's height. Her right ankle was affixed to mine and pulled me off balance as she struggled to deny entry to Diskare's hand. I struggled as the chain above pulled tightly against the gag in my mouth wrenching my neck. Diskare had apparently moved from a caress to a more painful stroke with his hand as the young blond began to whimper and moan more loudly. Diskare laughed, "She'll do. Unchain her."

Diskare pulled back as two men in red jumped forward to obey their leader's command. The girl's ankles were freed and she was pulled out of the line. My ankle was reattached to the next girl in the line, as the line was slid together to fill the gap. I watched as the blonde was led to the black leather divan which had been set before us. Diskare approached her and stroked her hair gently. She stood an inch or two above him.

I could see his expression turn from admiring, almost gentle, to hard and fearsome as his mind contemplated the crimes he had in store for this poor creature, and, inevitably, for the rest of us, dangling like meat, ready for the butcher. Some dark hatred was welling up inside him, some need to hurt, to humiliate, to punish. The blonde girl stared back at Diskare in wonderment and fear. She could see it too.

"And now, my pretties," Diskare turned to us, "you will begin to learn the lessons of your new life. Your sister in bondage here will demonstrate how pain can motivate. Will you not my darling?" He lifted her chin with his hand, pinching her face, leering. A moment's pause as his rhetorical question sank in to the blonde's consciousness. With a look of disdain, he motioned to the two men who had taken the blonde from the line. Without ado the girl was dragged to the front of the rectangular divan, her back to us. She was then forced backwards on the black leather, her hands, released from the belt around her middle and refastened to rings above her head set in the divan's side. Her legs were pulled up, her ankles fastened to rings on either side of her head. This placed her rear and sex in the air, elevated above her face, exposed, vulnerable; a shocking view and a harsh reminder of the parts of our bodies, heretofore protected, private, shielded from view, which would soon be open to any who desired to possess them, to dwell there.

Diskare approached the girl, running his hand down along her thighs to her sex. The little lips were pursed out slightly, peeking through the thin, pale downy cover of hair. Her anus gaped, hairless and pink. It was clear the girl was struggling to contain her discomfort as she was stretched beyond normal limits, her whimpers and moans audible, although faint. Her attempts to deal with her predicament caused her body to rock backwards and forwards in a pitiful imitation of the sexual act, as if some invisible lover were plunging into her. Diskare pressed his hand into her sex, now inches from her face, forcing his way past the delicate lips, inside. Two, three and then four fingers, he caressed and stroked her vagina, cooing softly in the girl's ear.

Diskare stood to one side, clearing my view as I dangled helplessly, my attention riveted on his hand. I, and I am sure my fellow prisoners, could see it, buried to his knuckles, now moving freely in and out of the blonde's sex. We could also see the girl's face as she looked up watching her own violation, her mouth obscured by the gag, but her

face and eyes contorted, graphically displaying her discomfort and humiliation.

I had certainly never seen a woman in this position and
never had witnessed anyone caressing a woman's sex before,
even my own. I was repelled but fascinated by the tableau.
After a minute, I could see Diskare's hand move back and
forth more easily as the girl's vagina, in an act of self
preservation and defense, became lubricated to accom-
modate the invasion. He then moved his hand to the other
entrance, her rear, and pushed into that portal, his way
eased by the juices from the girl's sex. She began to howl
beneath her gag, her voice strained and suppressed, but the
meaning unmistakable: pain and humiliation, nothing she
could have ever imagined, ever expected would be her fate.
Her debasement was more than symbolic, it was actual. She
was no more than a vessel, condemned to carry the objects
of desire, her tits, her pussy, her ass, destined to give them
up, open them, use them, at a master's whim.

Tiring of his exploration of the girl's openings, Diskare
leaned over and unfastened the gag from the girl's mouth.
Tears were streaming down her face. Diskare smiled at her,
the smile of a snake. "Are we comfy?" he asked with false
solicitousness. The girl struggled to contain herself, holding
back the pleas for mercy, the cries of despair. Diskare,
grabbed her face, "Answer me, dog."

The girl found her voice, "Please, oh please don't do
this. Please don't hurt me, please, I've done nothing, I'll do
whatever you want, please don't hurt me." Her voice
whining, signaling her loss of composure, her desperation.

"Ah, but my little slut, you will do that anyway. And I
think you and your friends here need a little lesson in how
we can inflict pain. It may save them later when they have
even a wisp of an impulse to disobey, to withhold what is
ours. No, I'm afraid you will have to be whipped now. But,

please feel free to beg and scream as much as you like. It will add to our enjoyment."

As Diskare stepped back, the girl's face contorted in fear. She continued to beg and plead for mercy, forgiveness, anything she thought might influence this man to refrain from a violent and unprovoked assault. Her voice pierced the stillness of the room. Diskare was handed a long, slender leather switch by one of the red shirted men and stepped back. He examined it thoughtfully, as if debating at how best to apply it to the subject which lay spread-eagled, quartered below him. A moment later the switch whistled through the air, landing on the girl's thigh with a loud 'crack!' A moment of disbelief and then the blonde screamed in pain. He struck her again and again, each stroke eliciting a screech of pain. Twelve times, the lash whistled through the air and landed on her exposed rear and legs. Several of the blows struck across her sex and her exposed, rear, brown star. Her screaming modulated. As each blow landed it would reach a crescendo, leveling off between blows, but never ceasing, never resting.

Diskare seemed to measure the blows carefully, landing each one apart from the last or other prior blows, striking at a different place or at a different angle each time. Little strings of welts rose on her thighs, with beads of blood oozing here and there, a testimony to the force with which the switch was administered. The room seemed too small to contain the girl's screams.

The effect of this on me and, I am sure, the entire line of women watching was electric. There could be no question but that for the whim of the moment, any one of us could be presently strapped across that very divan, measuring our tolerance for pain against Diskare's ability to inflict it. It was also clear that sooner or later we would be splayed    before    some    master    and    beaten,    tortured, tormented as was this woman before us. The whole line rocked back and forth as the women, including me, unconsciously swayed side to side, back and forth, attempting to contain our fear, tears streaming down our cheeks.

I looked at the woman Carla, as she stared at the display. Her eyes were afire, some secret lying there, achieving satisfaction and comfort in the young blonde's pain. Suddenly her gaze lifted and shot over to me. She had asked for me, to train me. I knew I had reason to fear her. I would struggle desperately to please her, I knew. And from her look I knew she would take great pleasure in making me beg and plead for mercy beneath her whip.

Finally the blows stopped. Diskare stepped back, a line of perspiration running down the side of his face. The girl's screams subsided into mere cries and then, whimpers. But if she thought her torment was over, she was mistaken. Diskare signaled to one of the red shirted men who, grinning, pulled open his trousers and released his cock. It was hard and thick and, without hesitation, he stepped forward, straddled the divan and pushed it into the blonde's gaping purse.

The cries began again as she pleaded with him to stop. His body slapped against hers, further battering her sliced and tender thighs and rear. He soon finished and was replaced by another and then a third. A fourth pushed himself into her rear, causing renewed screams of pain. All the while Diskare sat in his chair, facing the spectacle, smiling, savoring the girl's fate. The two servant girls knelt to either side of his chair, offering their breasts to him which he absent-mindedly caressed.

The dim lights gave a dream like quality to what was happening before me. The shadows played back and forth as the figures moved around the room, the men standing, waiting their turn, or wandering to the sides, their forces spent. Finally, after the sixth man had spewed his seed into the poor girl's flesh, Diskare rose again. The girl was moaning softly as he approached her. He leaned over her face, his face inches from hers, smiled at her and whispered something that made the girl wince. He then shoved home the gag which he had removed before and then turned back to us.

"A clear enough demonstration, my lovelies? Do you need more?" He approached the line, walking again back and forth like a cat. He stopped before a small, but well endowed, brunette. At the snap of his fingers the poor girl was released from the line. She was pulled forwards by Diskare using the ring on her gag. He pulled the gag upwards, forcing the girl to her toes. It was clear she was terrified as her eyes were as wide as saucers. Diskare caressed one heavy breast and then the other, obviously pleased with her ample proportions. The girl's hand squirmed in the bracelets which bound her hands to her sides, struggling fruitlessly to defend her self. Diskare lowered her down from her toes and looked her in the eyes.

"Well my sweet, what do you think, are you ready for a little dance with me?" The girl practically choked in her effort to plea for mercy from behind her gag. I knew what she was saying, what any one of us would be saying, what we certainly would end up saying, if not now, then later, begging for mercy, offering anything in exchange for the avoidance of pain. It was this girl's turn to beg now, if she got the chance.

Diskare turned magnanimous. Stroking the girl's breasts, pulling at her nipples, pinching them, he murmured "I tell you what slave, I'll give you a choice. You can suck my cock or you can take this slut's place on the divan. Which will it be my pretty?"

The girl frantically nodded, desperate to communicate her choice, blubbering from behind her gag, terror in her eyes. What could possibly have prepared any of us for this development in our lives? Were we expected to stand stoically and take our blows, whatever could be dished out against us, to resist? It was clear to me and I'm sure the other five captives who had witnessed the torment of the blonde girl before us that resistance was futile. If pain could be avoided, searing, burning pain, unnecessary violent pain, what was the real choice? Our bodies were out of our control. These men owned us, controlled us by right of possession and could do with us as they wished. That had just been demonstrated.

Opening our bodies to their fingers, hands, tongues or cocks was not optional. Should we withhold that which could be taken from us at any time? As had been demonstrated to us a moment earlier, the use of our bodies was not something that would depend on our consent or co-operation. What difference then if we could use our bodies to limit pain, avoid it?

Diskare pushed the brunette to her knees and loosened the gag, pulling the cock-like shape from her mouth. He pulled his stiffened manhood from the slit in his pajama like trousers and waved it in the girl's face. Hungrily, the girl pounced on it. She worked heartily, bobbing her head back and forth, kissing the knob, licking around the tip. Her hands were denied her, but she sucked earnestly, her eyes shut, as if to force out the dismal reality of her plight. After all, a cock could be anybody's.

Diskare leaned back slightly as his eyes closed to slits. The room was again quiet except for the sounds of the brunette struggling at her task, small cries and moan slipping out as she pleasured her master. Diskare then grabbed the back of the girl's head and took control. With his fist full of hair, he pulled and pushed her head back and forth, jamming his cock to the back of her throat, pulling it out again to the very edge of her lips. Suddenly, his body jerked, he grunted and pulled violently against the girl's head, forcing all of his flesh deep into her mouth. And then it was over.

The girl was released, crying, gagging, as she slumped to the floor. The men around the room laughed at her distress. Diskare pulled his tool back into his pants and turned to Carla. "Have the rest whipped and then released to the men for some fun. You may take this one with you," indicating me. "I'll take charge of the little one and send her back to you in the morning."

Carla nodded and snapped her fingers to transfer the command to the men who stood about the room. She pointed to the brunette on the floor, "And this one, Mr. Diskare?"

Diskare laughed, "Just give her five strokes on the breasts, she deserves some consideration for her efforts. But tomorrow, send her around and I'll think up something nice."

"As you say, Mr. Diskare," she replied. The small girl at the end of the line, the little teenager, was released from her chains and leashed. Diskare pulled her unceremoniously behind him as he left the room. Two of the men had already raised the brunette from the floor and replaced her gag. Her hands were released from her sides, only to be affixed to a chain from the ceiling.

Quickly, five sharp blows from a riding crop were delivered across her breasts. She danced and spun, attempting to avoid the blows, whimpering and sobbing behind her gag. The taller of the two men who had chained her hands above her, was clearly practiced and expert at his task as he awaited each shot with care, landing each one across the breasts as ordered, circling the girl first one way and then another to catch her just right. It seemed a familiar game to him, amusing to his cohorts.

The brunette was released and pulled into the arms of a heavy set, light skinned fellow. As he led her away for use, another girl was released from the line and fastened, hands above her head. This time the blows fell all over her body, her thighs, her stomach, her rear. Each crack of the riding crop brought a moan and cry from behind the gag. Twenty blows in all for her, and then the next girl and then the next. I stood alone watching the last girl but me dance a lively step as the blows fell across her body. I was sweating down my arms and chest, my knees were weak. I felt that I wouldn't be able to stand the blows. But for one time, I had never been struck in anger.

As the brunette was handed off to one of the red shirted men for fucking, the woman, Carla, came up to me. I cringed with fear as she approached me. She took hold of my right nipple and gave it a cruel, hard squeeze. The pain shot into me like a bolt of lightning. I moaned through my gag.

"It's time for us to go," she said to me. "We're going to have some fun of our own."

She released my left leg from the girl next to me and then freed my gag from the chain that led from my gag to the ceiling. I felt my knees go week as she led me by the leash affixed to my collar to the door.


To be continued....